In Bed With Luca

This edition is published by Prime Enterprises Media s.r.o.

First Edition

ISBN

978-80-90-9552-0-2 (PDF)

978-80-90-9552-4-0 (PAPERBACK)

DEDICATION

To the One Who Inspired It All
For my lover, my best friend, and my greatest muse.

Table Of Contents

INTRODUCTION

I've had toxic boyfriends—charming at first, but ultimately draining, manipulative, and self-absorbed narcissists. For a long time, I kept my eyes shut in the relationship.

I couldn't understand why I kept attracting the same kind of men. Why did I fall for them? What patterns were repeating? Driven by these questions, I began studying my situations, emotional immaturity and narcissism—its behaviors, motivations, warning signs, and psychological roots. I dug into why narcissists act the way they do, why they hurt the people who care about them, and why they rarely, if ever, see themselves clearly enough to change.

The father is the one who shapes our adult romantic life. We keep seeking copies of him—even if you shake your head in disbelief now, it's true. He plants this pattern deep in our subconscious. The only solution is to start searching in different waters. The ones that may seem boring, scary, or unfamiliar. But in my experience, this was the only way forward.

This book is the result of that journey—my attempt to share what I've learned, not only for my own clarity but to help you recognize red flags early, protect your energy, and avoid wasting time on someone unwilling or unable to face themselves.

Chapter 1:

Luca's Childhood

Luca Santoro always felt destined for more than the narrow alleys and sluggish afternoons of his small hometown in southern Italy, nestled in the heart of Apulia. Born in a modest seaside village as the youngest of four brothers, he grew up in a family where tradition wasn't just valued—it was law. His father, a fisherman, often grew upset for no apparent reason, but Luca never heard him apologise.

Luca's mother, confined to the walls of their home, harbored ambitions far beyond her own life, placing them squarely on his shoulders. She dismissed his dreams as childish illusions while demanding her own be fulfilled without question. Having never studied, she ruled the kitchen as her kingdom and poured all her hopes into Luca. When tears welled in his eyes as a boy, she cut them off with a sharp command: "Boys don't cry." A poor grade drew swift judgment, her disappointment sharp and unforgiving. No matter how hard he tried, he could never seem to be enough. Good behavior, stellar report cards, small triumphs—all were merely expected. But one misstep, one stumble, and her criticism fell heavily upon him. Relentless, watchful, exacting, she rationed her love through rebuke. If there was a contest, Luca was expected to win; if there was a standard, he was to surpass it. He became her final hope, the vessel for redeeming her own unfulfilled dreams.

Acceptance came only in moments of flawless performance, when Luca bent himself into the shape his mother demanded. And so, he grew to believe her love was conditional—a prize earned only through perfection. Under this burden, he set lofty goals to prove his worth. Yet they often ended in crushing disappointment—plans not thought through, dreams pursued at the wrong time, outcomes falling short of expectation. Achievement alone defined him, but it was never enough. He never learned to break his ambitions into smaller, gentler steps. When he failed, as he inevitably did, the verdict inside him was merciless: he was nothing.

He would never forget that morning. A small boy, standing at the doorstep with his brown schoolbag in hand, ready to leave but carrying a weight in his chest he couldn't yet name. "Don't forget what I told you," his mother called from the kitchen. "Bring home at least one A today. And no foolish behavior."

"Yes, Mom," he said softly.

"Did you say yes, Mom?" she snapped.

Luca swallowed.

"Yes, Mom," he said quietly again.

At school, it wasn't much different. His teacher called on him again. "Luca, read the sentence out loud," she said, pointing to a line in the book. The word quickly stared back at him like a trap. He froze.

"Y-ickly..." he stammered. The class burst into giggles.

"Did you hear that?" the teacher scoffed.

"Y-ickly! My God, child, this isn't French—it's Italian! Say it again," the teacher asked, smiling.

"Rrrrapidamente," he repeated, his cheeks burning.

The laughter cut through him like a blade. He didn't speak again that day. At home, silence reigned. That evening, his father returned early from the docks. Luca sat at the table, eyes fixed on his textbook, the pages blurred by tears he refused to let fall. His father looked at him, then at his mother.

"What happened?" he asked, his voice curt.

"Some nonsense at school," she shrugged.

"What kind of nonsense?" his father pressed.

"Says they're laughing at him. Can't pronounce his R's." Luca's stomach knotted. He braced for his father to mock him, too. But instead, the man stood, pulled on his coat, and left without a word. The next morning, Luca was transferred to a different class. His new teacher was kind, his voice calm. No one laughed at him anymore.

But the shame, the wound, the silent ache—they stayed with him. Years passed, and while his brothers followed in their father's footsteps and turned to the sea, Luca felt drawn to something else. He was fascinated by stories of self-made men, by the glittering pull of faraway cities, and by the dream of becoming someone different. Then, during high school, his class took a field trip to Milan. As they stepped off the bus into the city streets, Luca froze. Towering storefronts, elegant people, design, light... His heart raced wildly.

"This is it," he whispered to himself.

"Here... this is where I belong."

That night, when he returned home, his mother was already seated at the table.

"How was the trip?" she asked without looking up.

"It was... beautiful," he replied carefully.

"Maybe someday I'd like to do something different. Something with fashion. Or start a business."

His mother raised her head. "What nonsense are you saying? You'll be a doctor. Or an accountant. Not some entertainer."

His father said nothing, but he bit the inside of his cheek, as always. Luca looked down at his hands—soft palms, untouched by the sea, not like his father's. He felt something inside him begin to die. So, he shut down. He studied late into the night and brought home perfect grades. His mother nodded, as if it were expected. One time, he brought home a B. She slammed his notebook on the table. "This is all you're capable of?" she hissed. Luca said nothing. The constant misunderstanding, the guilt, the judgment—it shaped him into a perfectionist, an overachiever. His drive wasn't fueled by passion, but by fear. Fear of failing her. Fear of being unlovable if he wasn't perfect. And the girls he met? They just wanted weddings, babies, and somebody to take care of them.

Luca realized that love, at least the way he understood it, would only slow him down. So, he closed off that part of himself. Love could wait. First, he had to prove himself—above all, to himself. Success, for someone like Luca, wasn't a gift from birth. It was a goal—one to be built step by step, risk by risk.

Chapter 2:

Benedetta

And then he met her at Cala Corvino Resort. While working as a lifeguard during summer break, he saw her unexpectedly and couldn't get her out of his mind.

The next day, he eagerly awaited her return. He watched as she lay in the sun, carefully applying oil to her toned, sun-kissed body. She came back every day, as it was her summer retreat. She didn't fall for his charm—she fell for the man behind the façade.

Benedetta saw more than Luca's handsome face. She saw through him—past the mask, past his smile, beyond the carefully constructed walls he had spent years perfecting. Her warmth was like sunlight after a long winter, a sharp contrast to the quiet, cold emptiness Luca had grown accustomed to. She craved real love, an anchor to lean on, a place where she could finally be heard.

In the home where she grew up, no one had ever listened.

No one had time for her thoughts, her feelings, her voice. They had money, but no time for her. Something inside Luca shifted. To earn more, he took a job at a vineyard near Fasano, so he could afford to take her out, buy her gifts, and learn about wines. She came from a wealthy family, and he didn't want to seem like the poor, uneducated guy. Her father, a businessman, sold wines from local vineyards abroad, while her mother managed the finances. For the first time in years, Luca felt it—a fragile, flickering hope. Maybe... just maybe... he could have that too.

But the truth Luca carried was heavy, complicated, and too painful. He feared revealing everything inside him: his hunger for power, wealth, and the recognition that had never come. He worried that if she saw the real Luca, she would leave. So, he told her what she wanted to hear, wearing the mask that made her feel safe. She sensed something was off—a subtle awkwardness—yet chose to believe in him and their love. But love wasn't enough.

Chapter 3:

Mr. Bellanti

It was another summer. Luca, now 18, watched the coast swarm with tourists as nightclubs pulsed until dawn. He worked as a seasonal DJ, spinning familiar tracks for Italy's holidaying elite. In those long, electric nights, he glimpsed their world: tanned businessmen arriving in luxury cars, clad in perfectly tailored linen suits, accompanied by women wearing diamonds like armor. One evening, while passing the VIP section where he worked, his eyes locked onto an impeccably dressed man surrounded by bodyguards.

Mr Bellanti, a titan of Milanese finance, is a name whispered in boardrooms and glossy magazines. Luca, sweating under cheap headphones and worn designer sneakers, did something bold: he approached a guard and asked for an autograph. To his astonishment, they let him through. Face-to-face with Bellanti, his heart hammered. Summoning every ounce of courage, he asked, "May I ask you something?"

The financier's lips curved into a curious smile, and he nodded. "What's the secret to your success?" Luca inquired. Bellanti leaned in, his cologne strong, his voice low and precise. "The secret," he said, "is setting goals so high they scare you and then chasing them until they don't."

In that moment, a spark ignited in Luca—a raw hunger, a flicker of inspiration. The path ahead felt less daunting. Soon after, with a battered secondhand suitcase in hand, Luca moved to Milan to attend university. By day, he attended lectures and studied textbooks; by night, he ruled as a DJ in exclusive hotel venues, surviving on strong espresso and adrenaline. His life became a blur of sound and ambition.

One evening, he received an invitation to a rooftop party at a luxury hotel. Inside the private suite—silk drapes, crystal chandeliers, and people unconcerned with price tags—Luca stepped into another Italy, not of pasta and pizza but of private jets and penthouses. The fashion elite took notice. Top models danced to his beats; famous designers nodded in approval. He was drawn deeper into this dazzling inner circle.

Villa cocktails by Lake Como, weekend yachts in Portofino, après-ski champagne in Cortina. But Luca didn't just want to observe; he wanted to belong from the inside.

He began composing music tailored for top-tier fashion events. Her death struck Luca like a blow to the chest. Grief and regret crushed him; guilt suffocated him. It wrapped around him like a fog. He had lost her—not just to death, but to the silence between them. He realized, too late, that no performance, no success, no fleeting encounter could replace real love. Haunted by what he'd lost, Luca faced a truth he could no longer evade. He had to change, or he would lose himself completely. So, he made a choice—no more feelings, only sex, runways, private showcases, and wild launch parties.

He reached out to designers and supermodels, offering his sound as the heartbeat of modern luxury. Beneath the glamour, tension simmered. He wasn't sure where he was headed, and he was too busy for Benedetta.

One day, she woke up and realized she was alone.

Despite all the dreams and hopes she brought to their relationship, no one truly cared. Luca was neither physically present nor mentally engaged. His attention was elsewhere; his actions misaligned with the words he had spoken. When she confronted him, he fell silent. His silence was deafening; his absence unbearable.

She wasn't seeking money or fame, but real love—a soft place to land with someone who would catch her when she fell. Yet all she found was emptiness. Loneliness consumed her as Luca grew more distant. Days passed when she felt unseen, unheard, unfelt. She began to disappear inside herself, feeling invisible.

And Luca, from his perspective, was loyal, but he never asked how she was. He posed questions but never truly listened. When she spoke of her dreams, he nodded politely but never shared his own. His silence, coldness, and distance left scars no one could see. And in her darkest moment... she took her own life. She had taken her own life—not because of Luca, but because she never felt seen. She spent her days waiting, living for others instead of herself, until she no longer wanted to live at all.

For Luca, this was a crushing heartbreak. Not only was he alone, with no one asking how he felt, but they also blamed him. Some people speculated that he had done something to her, and he could barely breathe there anymore.

Chapter 4:

Mr. Rossi

Perhaps by chance, or due to his doubts about DJing, Luca caught the eye of Mr. Rossi, a renowned designer, at a fashion show. Rossi took a liking to him and soon invited Luca to work as his assistant. Luca carried fabric samples and espresso, took meticulous notes during fittings, and absorbed everything—design techniques, color theory, fabric sourcing, and client psychology.

Luca's personal life spun as fast as his vinyl. He dated two models simultaneously, then briefly surrendered to the passion of a bisexual couple he met during Milan Fashion Week. When rejection came—especially from models who saw him as an outsider—he sought solace with escorts who resembled those he couldn't have. He wasn't searching for love, but for closeness.

Then one model, with whom he spent more than one night, offered an idea that changed everything.

"Why don't you launch a fashion brand for men like you?" she said one morning over breakfast in bed. "Men who weren't born rich but can look like they are."

He listened. While still working as an assistant, he launched a fashion line—sleek, sharp, unmistakably Italian, with a rebellious edge. A brand for the modern power player, dressed not just for success but to command respect. He poured everything into it—his savings, his vision, his name.

His first boutique opened in Bergamo, with Mr Rossi there to christen it. Milan was too expensive, too cutthroat; Bergamo offered stability, a solid foundation. Customers came quickly: local entrepreneurs, ambitious youth, curious tourists. A year later, he launched a second store in Milan, which turned a profit from day one.

Yet Luca remained unsatisfied. Success in Milan wasn't enough. He craved more. He aspired to be the next Gucci, the next Armani—a name recognized worldwide. But then he felt walls closing in. He hadn't come from the right family. He lacked the right surname. He didn't have an American passport. The Gucci era had long passed. While the fashion world applauded his ambition publicly, many ignored him in private. He was invited to parties in Italy, smiles and toasts all around. Yet the real deals—those made behind closed doors abroad—slipped through his fingers. "If the gate doesn't open for me, perhaps it'll open for someone else," he thought.

He adopted a new identity—Luc Santor—his ticket to global recognition. His life became a blur of private jet engines and silk boardrooms. He dated actresses, models, and influencers. Photographers captured him; critics praised him; rivals envied him. Still, nothing filled the void within. Despite his success, Luca wasn't at peace. Past failures haunted him like shifting shadows.

He couldn't see his accomplishments; instead, he replayed the boy who felt unworthy, the boy who failed in school, the boy who disappointed Mom, Dad, and Benedetta. He lived in the past, relived mistakes in the present, and feared them in the future. This cycle trapped him: successful on paper, yet drained, anxious, detached from reality. He focused more on what he'd lost than what he had or could gain. He chased perfection, believing it would bring fulfillment. But no wealth, travel, or fame could silence the fear inside him. He was no longer driven by ambition but by fear—fear of failure, fear of being small again, fear of disappointing himself, just as he had disappointed his mother. So, he schemed.

He convinced himself the answer lay in a strategic marriage to someone wealthy, respected, from the "right" circles—a way to ensure he'd never fall again. What he hadn't realized was that the boy he'd tried to outrun still lived inside him, chasing the same validation.

Chapter 5:

Wife

Luca devised a new plan. If he hadn't been born into the "right" family, he would find someone who could open those doors. He needed investors to back his ambitious, fast-growing business. He sought financial stability, strategic connections, and a final push to elevate his project further. He met Patrizia at one of his fashion shows, bathed in light, buzzing with energy.

She was introduced as an investor with a sharp eye for potential—Ivy League-educated, daughter of an elite banking family. Elegant. Composed. With calm authority that made people pause. From the start, it was clear she'd be more than a financial partner. She possessed a rare blend of business acumen and refined grace, perfectly suited to the high-stakes world Luca aimed to conquer. Their collaboration began professionally. Her backing fueled his creative drive; his vision gave her confidence. Together, they forged a powerful alliance. Her discipline balanced his restless energy. His quick temper had often cost him relationships, deals, and trust in the past. But with her, he learned the value of patience, endurance, and thinking several moves ahead. She guided him through finance and long-term strategy complexities. He brought passion, edge, and innovation to their ventures. Over time, their partnership grew personal—rooted in mutual respect.

Marriage seemed a natural step. A merging of minds and ambition. Outwardly, they were the perfect team: a successful entrepreneur and a brilliant investor, navigating luxury with elegance and precision. She came from wealth; her assets were substantial. But at her lawyer's urging, Luca signed a prenuptial agreement, ensuring, in case of divorce, all property and holdings would revert to her. He accepted without hesitation, confident in their bond and shared future. But Patrizia knew he had once weighed her heart against his wealth. As more time passed, she had no respect left for him. No loyalty remained, no shared dreams—only her own vision guided her. And what he also didn't know was that she had taken out a life insurance policy, naming someone else as the beneficiary. Her family name carried weight, but her character defined her—resilient, composed, strategically brilliant. In her, Luca found a partner who challenged him, believed in him, and shared his vision for a future built not just on success but on clarity of purpose. Together, they moved forward—an ideal fusion of passion and precision. He thought he could control her fire, but gradually, something shifted. Her relationship with power ran deeper than Luca had expected. She craved control—and revenge—for his dishonesty, for not showing his full cards. She felt he never trusted her fully, so she decided not to trust him either—and acted exactly as he expected. Every move she made was calculated; she simply played his game, pretending all the while. She became a mirror of his dark side—his half-truths, manipulation, desire for power, and material success. When

Luca raised concerns that hurt or confused him, she often dismissed them.

"That never happened," she'd say, calm as ever. "You're imagining it," she added, echoing the very words he once used on her. Her words blurred truth's edges, weaving uncertainty into their conversations until Luca distrusted his own memory. She maintained dominance not through shouting but through subtle erasure. She'd feign ignorance of contracts, logistics, and technicalities, only to handle them quietly, flawlessly, behind his back—not to help, but to remind him she could. Instead of open dialogue, there was silence. Long, punishing silences. Days of being ignored. She'd leave the room when he spoke, look through him as if he didn't exist. She didn't argue—she punished. And he didn't always know why.

Little by little, Luca questioned himself. Inch by inch, he unraveled, doubting his instincts, his worth, his place in his own life. It was insidious control—silent, invisible, creeping into his being's marrow until it was indistinguishable from his thoughts. He craved release, some fracture in the cage, some reminder of who he'd been before doubt took root in his mind's corners.

In his yearning's stillness, one name rose above others—Benedetta. He ached for her gentleness, her unguarded love, the raw, disarming honesty that once laid him bare and made him whole. At first, it was a whisper, a shadow passing through his mind's quiet. Then nights grew longer, filled with restless searches—not for pleasure, but for understanding, a fleeting echo of connection, a glimmer of recognition. Finally, in the hollow hours before dawn, he reached out to an escort, hoping to grasp some fragment of what he'd lost.

It wasn't lust—not really. It was something more fragile, more urgent: his aching need to be seen. He needed to feel he still had worth. She was a stranger, yet she listened without expectation or judgment. Her touch was deliberate, neither cold nor cunning—a quiet attentiveness honoring the fragility she sensed in him.

In her presence, Luca breathed freely in ways he hadn't dared for years. For the first time, the weight he carried—the silent, unyielding weight—felt almost liftable, if only momentarily. He felt like a person again—not a problem to solve, not a collection of failures and unmet ambitions. Just... himself. The quiet between them held a strange, tender weight. Each word, each gesture, soothed parts of him long ignored. Though he knew this encounter was fleeting, he clung to it, desperate for the reminder that he could still matter.

Yet after each encounter, he returned home with guilt lodged in his chest like a stone. But beneath the shame, something quieter lived too—a breath of truth where reality could exist as it was. A space where he could exhale, unquestioned.

Chapter 6:

Tanya: The Most Expensive Girl in Rome

Tanya had always been beautiful—too beautiful, some said, so beautiful that people whispered. In her village, beauty wasn't a blessing but a curse. Her father called her a whore before anyone had kissed her. Her brother watched her like something he could break. Neighbors whispered because men stared too long. At fifteen, she was already guilty in their eyes.

So, she decided. At nineteen, she would move to Rome. If they were going to shame her anyway, she'd become what they feared most—an escort model, not just any, but Rome's most expensive. At nineteen, she left with a small suitcase and quiet rage in her heart. In Rome, she joined the agency, transforming into the woman who dealt in ecstasy.

Only wealthy clients, high payments, refined behavior, and safe sex. By twenty-two, she'd bought her own apartment in Prati—sunlit, elegant, cold, like her heart. She told herself she was free—no man, no children, no one to claim her. She planned to savor life on her terms, to live richly, luxuriously, to die alone, unbound. But slowly, almost imperceptibly, something unraveled. Then it grew, insistent, painful. Relationships built on illusions held a sickness, a hollowness no charm or thrill could mask. Not even Luca noticed at first;

they were intoxicated by excitement. But eventually, a cold, unyielding void appeared, impossible to fill.

No words, gestures, or efforts could bridge the emptiness between them. Private moments with Tanya were perfect, technically, yet carried a shadow that lingered. It settled in the soul like black ash. Each time, Luca left with something hollow gnawing at him on a fine, invisible level—something that didn't breathe but suffocated. With her came restlessness, a quiet, creeping emptiness he couldn't name at first, like an echo in an empty room, a shadow on a clean wall. Tanya never spoke of her feelings. She didn't need to. She transmitted them through her body, through touch.

Luca didn't notice at first; on the surface, everything seemed fine. The body responded. Desire worked. He felt like a king. But inside, something crumbled. With each encounter, she left a fragment of herself in him—not beauty, not passion, but weight: unworthiness, old rage, deep fear, guilt, pain, silent despair. It soaked into him, invisibly, quietly, through the skin, through a closeness never real, only simulated by their bodies. And he, though physically satisfied, began to wither inside. Day by day, night by night, he couldn't understand why. With a prostitute, a man never leaves unscathed. He took more than experience and pleasure—her shadow, a dark, stagnant energy that neither heals nor breathes, lingering, suffocating slowly. Tanya was beautiful, painfully so, a woman who could silence a room with her presence. Yet her eyes were always elsewhere, never fully meeting Luca's.

She didn't believe in gentle things—love, honesty, trust. To her, they were fragile illusions, fleeting as smoke, easily shattered by disappointment. She'd learned the world dealt harshly with hope, so she kept her heart armored, her desires measured, her faith in goodness buried. She sought excitement to feel something in the endless echo chamber where her soul should have lived. That drew Luca in—the darkness, the mystery, not her look, but her wounds. Her past had torn her apart. A father who abused her, a brother who followed suit, treated her like furniture, an object. She was breathtaking, yet felt filthy, and worse: believed she deserved it. Once, Luca noticed scars on her slender arms—thin, white, tiny lines, quiet tallies of pain.

"When I was younger," she said with a half-laugh,

"I used to cut myself, just to feel what pain was. Not to feel the pain I had. But the pain never left; it simply changed form."

With every client, every night she sold herself, a piece of her slipped away. Each client brought her deeper pain, and she willingly embraced BDSM to feel even more. Pain was the only world she knew. She became a ghost in her own life, an observer behind glass, searching for proof of her worth from anyone, yet looking in the eyes of the wrong men. Men valued her body and passion, not her being. She surrendered to their hunger, and with each touch, self-loathing deepened. It was all she knew. Sex became a cruel stand-in for love. Luca gave gifts, compliments, and played the role of "good friend," a brief light in a world that had cast her in shadow. But he never offered what she truly needed: understanding, presence, respect, a helping hand.

She never asked, unaware of what could ease her weight. Until one evening, she surprised herself, asking him to take her to a swinger party.

"What's that?" he asked, barely interested.

"A sexy party for rich people, like in the movie with Tom Cruise and Nicole Kidman," she smiled, sadness outweighing hope.

"I want to go once, look like I have a normal, rich life too." Tanya never asked for anything, never begged. But this sentence... was a plea. So, he nodded, unsure what else to do.

Chapter 7:

Behind the Gate

The old iron gate opened as their car rolled onto the gravel drive. The newly built garage loomed ahead, sleek and modern against the villa's crumbling charm, but it was packed. A sunburned parking attendant in a faded vest approached, his Romanian accent unmistakable. Wordlessly, he took the keys and handed Luca a numbered ticket. Transactional. Quick. No questions.

They stepped into the heavy summer air, heading toward the villa—not just any swinger club, but one hidden behind wrought-iron gates on Lake Garda's shoreline, a 17th-century villa where candlelight flickered on marble statues and laughter echoed off stone walls. Here, Northern European strangers met behind masks, where outside rules dissolved. They called them candle nights for their atmosphere, concealed by ivy-covered walls and iron gates.

The villa stood like a fortress of indulgence. Marble floors gleamed beneath candle chandeliers, casting golden light across velvet drapes and antique mirrors. The main gate closed at seven, but guests still arrived, familiar with unspoken rules. Luca wasn't. He couldn't book a room.

"It's full," the event manager wrote after Luca booked the ticket. "But the wellness area has lockers and showers. You'll be fine." And Luca hoped they would.

Luca and Tanya needed masks and capes.

The hallway lacked air conditioning, only the slow churn of bodies waiting for over half an hour. Luca chose black velvet capes; Tanya picked the masks, shimmering faintly, mysterious, theatrical. They queued to pay, but the line moved painfully slowly. Hotel guests checked in at the same table, bypassing the formal reception. No passports, no formalities, just nicknames, keys passed discreetly.

The night began, yet Luca felt unease. Trusting his instincts, he kept his phone and wallet in a small bag, ignoring the suggestions of the staff — whether waiters, hostesses, or receptionists to leave them in the car or at reception. Inside, the atmosphere pulsed with quiet opulence. Men in sharp tuxedos, polished shoes echoing on marble, women in flowing silk dresses and Venetian feather masks. Everyone wore masks, some Venetian, some minimalist, to hide or become someone else. It wasn't vulgar.

It was ritualistic, luxurious, elegant, yet pulsed with primal need. Luca didn't grasp their objective. These weren't strangers from shadows; they knew each other, questioning newcomers. They were lawyers, architects, entrepreneurs—men who ran companies, raised families, built empires. Tonight, they arrived without lovers or escorts in designer heels. Scattered among them were real couples, mostly over fifty-five, seeking excitement, an escape from routine's slow quiet. Luca noticed no Italians except the servers working for the hotel, not the organizer.

At their table, Luca kept looking around, but disco lights flashed into his eyes. Tanya, disgusted by the performance—a German woman in black latex swallowing swords as candlelight danced on her outfit—sat stiffly. The next burlesque dancer's routine lacked spark. The dinner service was excellent. Fifteen round tables, each set for five couples, fostered mingling before the ceremony. Luca had no interest in socializing, especially as wine loosened tongues and adults acted like overexcited teenagers. When asked where he was from, he lied easily. He listened as table talk soured, casual jabs at Italians tossed with ignorant confidence. One man claimed Romania was known for "pasta with goulash." The Romanian guest stiffened.

"Pasta with goulash isn't Romanian," he said calmly, irritation clear. Luca sipped his wine, silent. Another man grumbled about check-in delays, dinner running late.

"In Switzerland," he smirked, "we have watches and do things on Swiss time." With a theatrical shrug, he added, "But we're in Italy, so things are different... time works differently too."

He missed the irony: the fault lay with the Swiss organizer, not the Italian one. A German man tried speaking German to Luca. Another addressed Tanya in English, ignoring Luca—a sting of disrespect. In southern Italy, men speak to men before addressing their women. Here, they let go, playing high-class society, driven by one goal: sex.

After dinner, the organizer invited everyone to the disco. A naked DJ spun German tracks; the crowd grew louder, intoxicated, restless. The gong signaled the ceremony's start. Guests were to change into underwear, but Luca and Tanya had no locker; the wellness area was closed, and rooms lacked lockers or showers, leaving them stranded. Women in expensive lingerie provoked the men. The crowd moved to the hot room where disco lovers danced. The music shifted—the haunting hymn from Eyes Wide Shut filled the air. The master, in a red cape, paced, watching intently.

His assistants, prostitutes and strippers, gestured for guests to follow into the garden, where a blonde stripper reclined on a bed, girls posing around her. A man in a white mask approached the master: "These are your gifts for tonight." After the ceremony, everyone was to follow into the villa's cellars. The rooms were small, the crowd large. The master led them to a chamber aglow with candlelight, a girl posing like a living statue.

In the next room, bartenders checked guests; bags were left on a bare shelf, unwatched. Guests dropped their belongings carelessly. Luca refused to abandon his bag, standing guard by the shelf. Tanya stayed, a quiet anchor. The room was dark, not opaque, light hinting at details. Beds and chairs were arranged haphazardly; people sat, anticipating something. Red and black leather flickered, feathers brushed polished surfaces, and gold-framed mirrors reflected fractured glimpses. Plush pillows, colors muted, softened the tense atmosphere.

Some couples, aroused, began rough sex, not love, just to be seen, to attract. The master moved to the third room; the crowd followed. Luca stayed seated. But soon, the master took Tanya's hand, leading her away. Luca's heart tightened. Tanya didn't return. Fear gripping him, Luca hid his bag under his cape, following to the third room. A masked musician played an electric violin, the haunting melody weaving through the heavy air. Inside, three large areas with beds stretched across, each crowded with naked people tangled in sex, eyes locked in watching and being watched, absorbed in the ritual. Chairs held more guests watching. Tables stacked with drinks completed the restless anticipation.

Luca found Tanya in the center, surrounded, lying on her back, licking one girl's clitoris. The girl, kneeling, was penetrated from behind by two men; a third roughly used her mouth. Luca understood what drew them: not chaos or indulgence, but the magnetic pull of being together in that moment. Unease washed over him. He slipped out to the garden, lit a cigar, and thought. People played roles, then vanished. But fate had other plans. They weren't meant to meet, much less grow close. Yet, in the jasmine-scented garden, they found each other. Paola, twenty-seven, a model from Milan with golden silk skin and untold stories in her eyes, wore red silk, no expectations. She'd arrived with a French photographer, a friend who'd asked a favor, and now he was inside with Tanya.

"What are you searching for?" Paola asked, voice low.

"Not searching, hiding," Luca said, eyes locked on hers, acting interested but cold.

They spoke of nothing and everything—art, desire, loneliness, power. Neither touched the other, but both felt the pull. An invisible thread tied them, its permanence unclear. Before leaving, she pressed her phone number into his hand.

"Here's my number. Call me if you want more than tonight," Paola whispered.

"Careful. I don't do more. But you look like a woman who doesn't take no for an answer." Luca replayed with a mysterious smile.

"Maybe. Or, I'm the kind who knows what she wants," Paola answered with an even more mysterious tone.

"And what do you want, Bella?" Luca asked playfully.

"You. But not just your body... I want your secrets, " Paola responded with a provocative smile.

He tilted his head, a slow grin spreading.

"Secrets are heavier than bodies, bella. Are you strong enough to carry mine?"

Paola leaned closer, her breath brushing his ear.

"I've carried worse. Besides..." She let her fingers circle the rim of his glass. "...the heavier the secret, the sweeter the confession."

He chuckled, low and dark.

"You're dangerous," she smirked.

"Dangerous is just another word for interesting." He swirled the amber liquid in his glass, eyes narrowing. "If I told you my secrets, what would you give me?"

She tilted her head, eyes locked on his.

"Everything you didn't know you needed. Everything you were too afraid to want."

He set his glass down, the sound cracking the quiet.

"You're playing with fire," she smiled, slow, deliberate.

"Good. I like the burn," he murmured, a teasing smile spreading across his face.

Without another word, she walked away, her hips' sway leaving tension, leaving him staring at the space she'd claimed. Luca's night wasn't about tomorrow, so he didn't respond.

He found Tanya, and they headed to the garage, moving through shadows.

The car was gone. Confused, Luca went to reception, where a Pakistani man, unlike the earlier attendant, spoke no Italian.

By 2 a.m., Luca was searching the grounds, guests shrugging, bleary-eyed, pawing at jackets and bags. Some thought the car had vanished. Frustration and anxiety gripped him. He called the police, who arrived efficiently, clipboards in hand, trying to order chaos. German guests, wobbling, confronted officers without passports.

Halting English from the police, fragmented drunken English from guests—no one understood each other. Frustration mounted. The scene teetered between chaos and farce. Backup arrived, police cars screeching. Officers stormed the swingers' room; the party ended. Music cut, laughter stifled, and intoxicated revellers stared at the law with guilty eyes. Some searched for nonexistent cars, others slumped, muttering complaints. Some hid in toilets, banging doors, locking themselves in. Others rushed to rooms, barricading themselves. Outside, escape attempts—climbing gates—ended with officers waiting. The night darkened: stolen cars, open windows, ripped-out radios, abandoned vehicles, missing bags, wallets lost in confusion. The police moved swiftly. The organizer's calm faltered; investigations linked her to prostitution rings and the Albanian mafia.

Luca watched with relief and disbelief. The villa's glamorous facade crumbled, revealing darkness. He lit a cigar, smoke curling as he exhaled, processing the night. The mask of glamour slipped, exposing a darker world. As dawn broke, Luca knew this was only the beginning. His car was gone. He called his cousin from Puglia, now a capo in a mafia family through marriage.

His cousin called back quickly.

"We found it," he said flatly.

"A few things are missing, but it's your car."

"We need to discuss conditions with them," he added.

"You pay, or we take it. But this could create problems."

Luca swallowed, the night's weight pressing. He nodded firmly.
"I'll pay. Just... bring it back," he said, determination cutting through fatigue.

His cousin paused, then nodded curtly.

"Fine. Consider it done."

Luca knew the debt would bind him in unforeseen ways; hiding it from his wife was nearly impossible. He ordered a taxi, took Tanya home, the atmosphere heavy with unspoken words. He resolved never to call her again, but Tanya's knowing glance said otherwise. She knew he'd return. She always knew they came back. But he didn't see the essential truth: Tanya hadn't just taken his time, an evening, a ride.

She'd taken his fragments, given him heavier guilt, a shard of her pain, proof of his failures. All that remained was guilt and anger, a weight he couldn't shake. Too late, his wife didn't follow blindly; she had them followed, waiting for the right moment. Patiently, revenge served cold. She'd arranged the car's theft—not for evidence, but amusement. She wanted to watch, catch him, make him remember. Exposing her own crimes was incidental. Then she struck, when it would hurt most—no yelling, no tears, just measured silence, disappointment, cold certainty. Every move calculated, every word premeditated, like a chess move. She'd stopped playing fair.

She was wounded with reason, craving more devotion, dominance. That morning, Luca came home tired. The apartment's air was heavier, hushed, like before a storm. His wife sat upright, calm, on the sofa. No tears, her eyes colorless, without warmth.

"I know," she said quietly, then fell silent. She said she understood mistakes, that he'd made one.

When he asked how to fix it, she replied, "Make me a child." She suggested it calmly, like a home renovation.

"Our child will fix everything, bring us back together, turn pain into reconciliation." Then she added the sentence that lingered for months:

"I'll forgive you... If you give me something only ours." She knew him too well, where to aim. He'd never wanted children; responsibility terrified him, a trap. But she knew the guilt—Tanya's slow-acting poison. So, he agreed—not from fear or love, but because guilt outweighs truth. Some men walk into traps rather than face the mirror before their hearts. That night, he gave her a child, like fulfilling a contract—regret and silent punishment. When it was over, they lay side by side, both alone, joined in body, separated in everything else. Outside, the rain fell.

Chapter 8:

Paola Rossini

Paola Rossini was always the center of attention, whether she wanted it or not. In her small town in northwest Italy's hills, people didn't just pass her; they turned. At school, at the market, stepping off the train—she made the world pause.

Her beauty wasn't quiet; it filled rooms, buildings. It made people nervous, fascinated, and envious. From childhood, Paola dreamed of stages—first as a singer, then a dancer, then a model—wherever the spotlight lived. But her mother, practical to a fault, crushed those dreams with iron logic: You won't like it. It's too expensive. It's not enough. The message was clear: Be less. Stay here. Be normal.

Paola was never meant for normal. She dressed differently from what locals expected. Her mother, a nurse at the local hospital, wanted her to follow suit. But Paola left for Milan as soon as she could, with a suitcase of thrift-store glamour and eyes fixed on the skyline. She enrolled in art school to keep a roof overhead, but her real education came in casting rooms, where beauty was currency, and competition was brutal. She stood in lines for hours to be seen for seconds, fighting jealous stares, whispered sabotage.

Backstage at fashion shows, models watched her like a threat—another flawless face amid fragile egos. Paola refused to play their game. She wouldn't flirt with agents or let producers "help" her for late-night invitations. She saw others meet "friends of friends" at elegant parties, fly to yachts for shoots unrelated to fashion. She saw contracts girls signed with agencies that owned them, dictating bodies, choices, and freedoms. Some models weren't just models; they were accessories, entertainers, sometimes darker—silent escorts in couture. But Paola drew her line. She chose the long road over the easy one, hard-earned, yes, over whispered invitations. She'd work harder, climb slower, never trading her body for shortcuts. Integrity was her armor, heavier than gold. She rose, not fully—a catalogue queen, polished face of mid-tier luxury. Glossy enough to turn heads, respected enough to get booked, well-paid, admired, and envied. But never crowned. Never the one. Always for a different reason: too Italian, not the right thing, not trendy enough, too much.

Agents smiled with empty eyes—one called her look too commercial, another too classy, not high fashion. Always a flaw, a technicality. Just when she reached higher, someone reminded her of limits, pushing her down gently, politely, like her mother.

The highest doors—covers, campaigns, Paris and New York runways—stayed closed. Paola told herself she had dignity, built honestly. But in her tiny Milan apartment, she wondered if honesty was just another word for unfinished. Paola had lovers, naturally. A woman like her wasn't unnoticed. Men followed with eyes, words, fantasies, but never truly saw her. They saw beauty that made heads turn, hearts skip, assuming vanity, danger, betrayal.

They called her a goddess, treated her like a threat. So, she hardened outwardly—a virtuous, rare, real woman, rooted but unsafe. Being soft scared her. She wanted something meaningful with someone strong.

Men couldn't win her; they had to earn her with consistency, integrity. But most seemed successful yet were weak, insecure inside, craving her as a prize, fearing they couldn't keep her, assuming she'd leave for someone better. As if beauty made faithfulness impossible. They held her at arm's length, tried to control or hurt her first. She couldn't find the right man—not because she was broken, but because her reflection intimidated fragile egos. Her strength, silence, and refusal to beg made them feel small. So, they left, lied, or stayed just to punish her for not needing them.

She feared wasting time on simple men, without vision. One man in Milan she loved—a dreamer, charismatic, lost actor—held her heart for years. They shared cigarettes on rooftops, whispered in train stations, and mapped futures in cafés that never closed. She believed in him; he claimed to believe in her. She stood by him in doubt, helped him rise—not loudly, but by being there, listening, advising, so others respected him, so he'd believe in himself. She supported his dreams, not for their perfection, but for him.

But he chose status over love, marrying a more famous, useful actress with a name that opened doors Paola had knocked on for years. It wasn't heartbreak that shattered her, but recognition: even love could be reduced to prestige. She'd lived his life, not hers, losing years. Paola decided against love. No promises with future betrayals. She'd have friends, flings, long nights, late mornings—nothing requiring faith, nothing giving power to hollow her. She called it maturity, but it was really survival and the fear of losing more of her heart. Especially with Italian men—beautiful, fiery, magnetic, knowing how to touch, whisper what bodies craved. The best lovers... and most dangerous liars. Kisses wrapped in poetry, betrayals in silk. She recognized the patterns: jealousy masked as protection, deep eyes promising everything, meaning nothing. Not all were bad, but enough were good at being bad. She had no time for deceivers. She built a circle of loyal artists, dancers, and expats—people who let her be herself, keeping things light, flirting without falling.

If love wanted her, it had to come without conditions, without an Italian passport. She'd given her heart once; he chose a red carpet. But Luca lingered in her mind, his look not just interest, but recognition, seeing through her curated charm to something raw.

Luca was distracted, sitting in meetings, nodding at clients, answering emails—nothing mattered. He saw her face turning away at the villa, her scent lingering like an unfinished sentence. He wanted to write her, the urge sharp, instinctive. But he hesitated—what if she didn't feel it? What if the connection was a trick of the night? Three days later, he messaged: "I haven't stopped thinking about you. Dinner at a luxury hotel? Something unforgettable."

She replied instantly, her pulse racing. He took her to a restaurant she knew, on the seventh floor of a luxurious hotel, offering elegant dishes amid black marble and backlit onyx, with superb Milan views. It was where powerful people dined. Luca watched her, memorizing every detail, every breath.

Tension crackled between them, each movement a dare. They spoke of work; she opened up, and Luca promised career help through contacts, pulling her in deeper.

They didn't last the night without touching. Luca had a room booked. Clothes fell like confessions; they gave in, all attention and energy. They didn't sleep, exploring each other with desperate urgency, erasing their loneliness. Luca was surprised by her hunger, boldness. Paola matched his rhythm, challenged him, pulled him into a storm he couldn't control. He took the lead; she let him. She loved his movement, dominance, and how he almost tore her soul with every thrust. At dawn, she slipped out quietly, careful not to wake him. Her heels clicked softly in the hallway, each step a fragile punctuation in the stillness, like closing credits of a film she never wanted to star in, a role not hers. She feared he wouldn't reach out, dreaded another disappointment. So, she chose self-sabotage, leaving before staying could break her.

She watched him go, carrying another fragment of her heart. She told herself it was over, the chapter closed. Yet, even as the words formed, she felt the weight of years surrendered, the ache of choices made for others, not herself. Each step away was liberation and confession—a silent surrender to a life waiting to be reclaimed, a heart to be pieced back together.

Chapter 9:

The trip

Two days later, Luca texted her again—another invitation, this time a lake trip. Brief. Impulsive. Perfect. A lovers' escape, he called it. Nothing serious, nothing permanent, just pure, undiluted pleasure. She arrived at the luxurious hotel to meet him, unsure but unable to stop. Before she could speak, he opened the luxury car's door, took her hand, and led her inside. The night was warm, clinging to summer's last breath as the cabriolet sliced through Milan's streets like a whisper in velvet. Paola sat in the passenger seat, hair wild in the wind, a laugh caught in her throat like champagne bubbles. Luca drove with one hand on the wheel, the other touching Paola's intimate spots.

The city blurred. Golden light reflected off polished storefronts; scooters darted past like neon fish. At stoplights, strangers stared, unsure if they saw celebrities or just two people defying rules. They shouted over the wind, made unfinished jokes, grinned at nothing, everything. Paola stood on her seat briefly as they sped along. They kissed at a red light—not from love, but because it felt possible. In that moment, they weren't models, entrepreneurs, or broken hearts in expensive clothes—just free, reckless, alive.

Driving into darkness toward the lake, hair tangled, they knew it was one of those nights. Luca turned off the main road silently, steering the cabriolet down a narrow lane flanked by trees, leaves flickering in headlights like confetti. City noise faded. Only tires on gravel, cicadas, and the slowing music, darker now.

He stopped beneath trees, the engine ticking as it cooled, air thick with the unspoken. Paola looked at him, half-smiling; he leaned over, brushing hair from her face with silk-like gentleness. There, in the hidden road's hush, he kissed her—not for show, not for cameras or jealous strangers, but quieter, realer, a slow, deliberate kiss starting at the mouth, reaching deeper, meant to linger, not repeat. His hands knew the path. Her breath caught. She shifted under his touch, recalling a language her body once spoke fluently. She didn't speak, didn't need to. Leather seats creaked; leaves rustled above, holding their breath. Wind slipped through the open car, cool against her warm skin, air charged with expensive perfume. When she came, it was quiet—a loud gasp into his neck, a shiver down her spine, a soft clutch at his shirt. Not performative, just real. Like something long awaited, now allowed. They sat, breathing in sync, the world still. Luca smirked, lips parted. "Best detour I've taken in years." Paola laughed, leaning back into the leather seat.

At the lakeside hotel, once the door closed, Luca lifted her onto the marble table by the window, kissed her like a starved man. No pleasantries, just heat, tension, two people knowing exactly what they needed. This wasn't love—something darker, dangerous.

"Don't fight it," he murmured, mouth near her pussy. "Just feel it." And she didn't, not just the physical, exquisite, but the surrender. He pleased her like he'd studied her in a past life.

Pressure, pause, pulse converged until she couldn't tell where she ended and his intention began. He watched, not with hunger, but fascination, as if satisfaction lay in showing her what she could feel. When her body tipped over the edge, it wasn't a ripple—a sudden, deep wave, out of control. She cried out, caught off guard, body slick with release, breath in sharp, shivering bursts. She reached for him blindly—chest, wrist, anything. He smiled, knowingly, not arrogantly.

"There it is, you showered me," he whispered.

For the first time in years, Paola felt seen, not just desired for beauty—completely, unapologetically.

The next morning was calm, sunlight dripping like honey over the marina, wind gentle, salty. Luca planned a boat trip, light, indulgent, just them, drifting along the coast, like a perfume ad. But at breakfast, his tone shifted, casual but calculated.

"Someone from the hotel asked something strange," he said, stirring espresso. "A guest—a woman, traveling alone, husband away on business. They asked if she could join our boat." Paola's stomach clenched; she wanted the boat to be theirs, their hours, the sea. But she smiled, composed.

"Sure," she said. "Why not?" They met her at the dock.

The woman, in her thirties, average-looking, chatty, was Mira, a masseuse.

"I came to relax, ended up walking alone," she laughed, as if unbothered. "My husband works too much. He said I should enjoy myself." Paola nodded, watching her sunglasses reflect the water. Something felt off—not dangerous, just untrue.

On the boat, the conversation fragmented. Paola didn't want to talk to a stranger; Luca seemed torn between charm, detachment. Mira asked to join them for dinner—"if it's no trouble"—offering massages as thanks.

"I'm good," Paola winked.

"Very intuitive. I can make you melt," Mira said quietly.

Luca glanced at Paola.

"You love massages," he said gently.

"But only if you're comfortable," Mira added.

Paola hesitated, fearing an argument with Luca, then nodded. Later, in their room, lights low, windows open to the tide's sound, Mira arrived with oils, an oddly rehearsed air. She moved confidently, too confident for a wellness worker.

She skipped questions, sheets, and temperature. Her hands were skilled, but Paola felt tension. Then it shifted—Mira's touch turned suggestive, lingering too long. Her voice dropped, whispering near Paola's ear. "Would you mind... if I kissed you?" Paola stiffened, heartbeat racing—not with desire, but confusion. She met Luca's unreadable eyes briefly. Mira waited, smiling. Curious, Paola let the kiss happen—soft, gentle, harmless—but it turned to licking Paola's body, feeling wrong.

"No," she said, quietly, firmly, sitting up, the sheet falling. "I don't like it."

Silence cut sharply. Mira smiled apologetically, too smooth, and packed her oils without protest. No one spoke much after. Luca poured a drink; Paola took a long shower. The lake moved, indifferent, endless. Paola wondered—whose idea was it? She carried the weight of disappointing Luca.

Days after returning to Milan, the memory lingered—silent, sharp as a knife. Their conversations grew sparse, heavy with the unsaid, as they prepared for New York. Paola sensed Luca hid something—not outright lies, but not truth either, not about his pregnant wife, carefully curating a single man's illusion. He couldn't open up, reveal sadness, or regret.

Luca lived between truth and omission, not lying directly, but shielding with silence. Behind it, his pregnant wife, a life elsewhere, responsibilities unnamed. Not dishonesty bound his tongue—fear. Terrified Paola would leave if she saw him fully, he kept her close, at arm's length—offering warmth, never the full truth. His intimacy was measured, calculated, enough to hold her, never enough to risk himself.

Chapter 10:

Home

Milan, near midnight. Luca returned home late from work, the city still humming with restless energy. He dropped his keys on the table, the echo louder than it should have been. For a moment, he stood in the half-light, caught between exhaustion and thoughts he'd tried to outrun all evening. The hallway was silent, only the refrigerator's distant hum and the wall clock's ticking were audible.

His wife sat in the kitchen, back to him, hunched over her phone. She didn't turn when he entered, didn't look up, didn't speak. This silence wasn't ordinary—not the quiet of two people beyond words, but a weapon. They hadn't spoken in days, not for lack of things to say, but because she chose silence. With every glance away, every exit from the room, she conveyed disapproval, perhaps pain. Luca didn't know if she knew exactly, but he felt her suspicion. Her silence, every omission of his name, carried the weight of unspoken judgment. Luca responded as he knew how—staying longer at work, burying himself in paperwork, losing himself in conference rooms, deals, emails, escaping into a silence he could choose. At work, there was peace. No one judged him silently to his face. But instead of remaining the steady, composed leader he was meant to be, Luca sought solace in employees, his conversations turning personal.

He spoke of his wife, her faults, his entrapment, rules he claimed he never agreed to. Quiet venting became a litany of grievances. Doubt crept into the team. Whispers circulated in hallways, over coffee breaks: Was he the strong, decisive figure they'd followed, or had his wife been steering his life? Some wondered if Luca's carefully constructed image—handling crises with calm authority—was a mask. The atmosphere shifted, imperceptibly at first, then palpably. Meetings grew heavier, decisions second-guessed, subtle alliances formed. Employees, once admiring his confidence, now hesitated, unsure whose guidance to trust. The man they'd seen as their leader cast himself as a victim, floundering under invisible burdens. The team, torn between comforting and holding him accountable, drifted.

Luca didn't notice.

Meanwhile, Paola thought of Luca. Maybe if she showed openness, daring, things would feel right again. That's when she got a bold idea.

"What if... we meet someone in New York?" she asked one evening over text message.

"Someone?" Luca texted back.

"A girl. Just for fun. One time," Paola wrote quickly, waiting for his reaction.

"You'd do that?" he answered immediately.

In her reply, she just sent a heart.

Chapter 11:

New York

The flight touched down at JFK under a gray sky, rain streaking the window like warnings Paola refused to read. She told herself this was the beginning of deeper trust. They found her online and chose her together—a sexy woman with large breasts and a full figure, not quite what Paola had imagined. She wasn't stunning, but had a calm, almost gentle presence. Luca arranged a suite in a luxury hotel, with champagne waiting.

When the woman arrived, Paola hesitated. Looking at her, she felt no desire, but pity. This woman didn't fit the fantasy—she was real, too wounded. But Paola played along with Luca, protecting the image they shared.

In the room, the mood shifted. Luca took the lead, playful, charged, aiming for something wild, cinematic. But Paola stayed still, disconnected. When he whispered to the woman to "show her something special," Paola felt it snap. This wasn't freedom or desire—it was annoying.

"She's not a toy," Paola said coldly.

Luca turned to the woman with familiar charm, as if to salvage the mood, make her feel special. He kissed her nipples, fingers touching her clit.

But Paola didn't like that either. Why should his energy, attention, seduction belong to another, even briefly? Then, as if he hadn't crossed a line, Luca shrugged at her.

"Don't be selfish." No softness, no irony—just accusation, delivered calmly, measured. Paola blinked. The word hit harder than expected. Selfish? She didn't even have to consider it. How can you be selfish toward someone whose purpose is to fulfill your needs—especially if you're paying for it?

She'd opened herself, allowed a stranger into their night, all to please him. Now she was selfish? He wasn't sharing an experience—he was controlling it, stretching her love's boundaries until they snapped.

Something in her did, quietly, inwardly, like a thread pulled too tight. She watched him—the way he smiled, his hand brushing the woman's breast. It wasn't fun anymore, but something deeper, unnameable, stinging. Paola realized it wasn't jealousy, but colder disgust. Paola faced the woman. "I'm done here. You should leave."

Silence. Confusion. But the woman understood, gathered her things quietly, and left.

Paola stared at Luca. "What the hell was that?"

Luca didn't answer. Luca remained silent, adopting the role of the victim: the one who had paid, yet was somehow being blamed. He poured himself a drink and stared at New York's skyline.

The next day, sensing Paola slipping away, he grew cold but changed course. He made her fall for him again, listening intently, feigning understanding of every word. They set new directions, boundaries for their fragile relationship. Luca shaped plans for their future, talking of bringing Paola into his world—working together, establishing a Rome modeling agency focused on male models, vital for his business. It promised partnership, ambition, and shared purpose. He vowed they'd build a future—side by side, partners in love and work, creating a life they'd once only imagined.

Paola liked the vision. Maybe he believed it. Or maybe he wanted it all: his world with Paola, a devoted wife, a family, a thriving business. He wanted it all, refusing to surrender even a fraction. Giving something up? Not for him. Winners didn't do that, at least not in his way of thinking.

Chapter 12:

Isolation

Meanwhile, Patrizia quietly wove a plan of isolation—not just professional, but physical. Her significant investment in Luca's business enabled new stores and international expansion. By now, they had branches in New York, Dubai, Monaco, and Paris, with more planned.

Drawing inspiration from Marco Zucchero's approach, she reshaped her role into that of an investor and strategist. She raised capital, closed lucrative deals, and systematically increased the company's value, presenting Luca with an image of shared success and a thriving business. She moved with precision. The capital increase wasn't quick, but a carefully orchestrated operation spanning months. Her first step was to reorganize the company's ownership structure.

Her silent shareholding soon became a decisive power. Then followed discreet meetings with employees and suppliers, who trusted her calm, analytical approach over Luca's impulsiveness. She spoke their language—measured, confident, armed with numbers. Through convertible bonds and direct capital injections, she secured new resources without relinquishing control. The company's value soared, not only from the expanding international network but also from the stability she cultivated. Luca, caught up in grand openings and media interviews, barely noticed the shift. On paper, it was a joint victory. In reality, the scales tipped quietly in her favor.

Pregnant, her moods shifted rapidly; she wanted Luca to care for her more. But his mind lingered on Paola. Patrizia felt his mind wandering and seized the opportunity to manipulate him. She started by playing the victim, then carefully seeded the notion that his few friends were a corrupting influence, out to destroy him. When that failed and Luca remained lost in thought, she provoked arguments, making clear who'd paid for his life, claiming that without her, he was nothing. Instead of drawing him closer, she pushed him further away.

Luca felt trapped, bound, powerless. The more she controlled the situation, the more his mind escaped to Paola—a world free of pressure, pain, or restriction. Yet she sensed his distance, and a new plan took shape: Luca should take more responsibility for their child while she assumed a more active role running their company.

After reorganizing the ownership, she transferred the company into a trust, specifying the trustee and beneficiary for after her death—definitely not Luca.. The words were simple, their weight lingering long after. Luca, who'd assumed he was indispensable, was quietly excluded from the future she planned without him. It was a boundary drawn in stone, a quiet assertion of control over a life too often hijacked by others' expectations. Deep inside, she felt sharp satisfaction.

Chapter 13:

The rules we break

She entered his life like sudden light—unexpected, impossible to ignore. With her, everything felt sharper—colors brighter, sounds fuller, air heavier with possibility. Luca knew desire, but this was different—not just longing, but immersion, a surrender to love's delicate, intoxicating pull. Her laugh echoed in his chest.

Every touch, every glance carried weight, thrilling yet terrifying. He wanted to claim it, hold it, yet knew love wasn't controllable. It was fragile. For the first time, Luca saw that losing it made it worth everything. Meetings with Paola were electric, secret, intoxicating, dreamlike. She stirred in him emotions unlike anything he'd ever known, a vibe that consumed his thoughts and left him craving more.

Luca never spoke of his life beyond those walls; Paola never asked. Part of her feared the truth; another was terrified the spell would break, their fragile, burning connection vanishing if named. Probing risked destroying its intensity.

She feared losing something beautiful, unwilling to risk more. As long as he touched her, whispering her name like sin and prayer in one breath, it sufficed. Yet unease lingered. Paola felt she was doing something wrong, even without cause. Luca circled back to her words, subtly accusing, picking at old wounds. He scolded her for flossing in the bedroom, claiming she changed her mind too often.

When she asserted her right to change her mind, his voice turned cold, sharp, threatening silence, abandonment: "Then find your own clients." He bought her things—his choices, not hers—clothes and gifts mismatched to her style, dressing a version of her in his mind. Decisions, big or small, ignored her opinion. It wasn't generosity—it was control dressed as care.

His boundaries shifted with his mood; words mismatched actions. Paola tiptoed, walking on eggshells, never knowing what might trigger him. He couldn't share what he truly loved, except work, fearing intimacy.

He kept things surface-level, avoiding deeper conversations and emotions. Hiding feelings maintained his control over Paola and the situation. Unable to handle emotions healthily, he responded with anger, sarcasm, and distance, carrying unresolved issues—his wife, inner conflicts—blocking building healthy relationships, not just with Paola. He loved discussing work, impressive experiences, and feeling safe. Elsewhere, he felt inferior, hiding weaknesses and vulnerability.

Paola memorized his repeated stories; no new ones came. He spoke for hours, uninterested in dialogue, leaving after speaking—or sex—without cuddling, without open conversation. Paola numbed slowly. In quiet moments, his softened, sleeping face seemed unreachable, innocent, yet doubts crept like smoke.

But one day, when she spoke to another model who knew Luca, the conversation turned to the event that Luca and Patrizia had attended. Paola had not been invited. Curious, she searched for a video to see if what she had heard was true. Then it appeared—a random YouTube autoplay: Rome's charity gala, elegant couples, rehearsed smiles. There was Luca, beside a tall, elegant woman with piercing green eyes and flawless posture. His hand lingered on her back, the gold of his wedding band catching the light. Both wore rings, and together they looked like the happiest couple alive.

Paola couldn't breathe—chest tight, heart racing, headache flaring, neck muscles tense. She watched it three times. The caption confirmed: Luca Santor, venture capitalist, with his wife at the Art for Change Foundation dinner.

Wife? She felt sick—not just from the lie, but her lack of surprise. She'd ignored the red flag signs: silent phone, vague answers, disappearances.

Paola texted: "You lied."

Hours later, no apology: "I didn't lie. I just didn't tell you everything. You didn't ask." Rage, betrayal, and shame tangled like barbed wire.

"You're married."

"My wife and I are like strangers," he wrote. "With you, I feel alive. Complete."

Paola stopped listening. Days in bed, unable to eat, sleep—not missing him, but hating herself for believing the fantasy, falling for someone not hers. It wasn't betrayal that hurt—it was the ache of still wanting him. She scrolled past his daily messages without a word: *"Thinking of you." "I'm sorry."*

Paola stayed with her friends. Yet she remembered Luca holding her hair when she was sick from wine, searching for pills for her headache, massaging her sore back, legs. Not seduction—care. Not their arrangement of lust, sex. So, she replied, intending closure, but agreed to meet near the Spanish Steps. Luca looked sleepless. He reached for her hand; she didn't stop him.

"I didn't plan to fall for you," he said quietly.

"You were an escape." She smiled bitterly.

"That makes two of us. I'm still married," he admitted.

"I know," Paola replied.

"But I can't stop thinking about you. I want more—not just sex, to be with you as planned in New York."

Paola wanted to walk away. Her body betrayed her, longing for his intensity, a drug. Something softer grew, untrusted.

"I don't do relationships with married men," she whispered.

"You do sex with them though," Luca said, voice low, rough with desire. "Maybe that's what this is. For now," he added.

She should've left, but didn't. She wanted more—not deep love yet, but something real, healing her past. Despite lies, Luca showed a raw, human side, craving danger, surrender, freedom his wife couldn't offer.

She followed that darkness, testing her edges with someone fearless. It wasn't reckless—it was ruinous.

Luca, drowning in a life he couldn't leave, felt a brittle hope, believing he could have both. He hid his child, offering fictions—divorce, grief, illnesses—for absences, silences. Truth was too heavy, messy. He feared she'd vanish if she knew. She wasn't meant to be the other woman forever. He pushed her away, cruelly, even as she reached deeper than anyone.

At first, Luca's attention, passion, intensity—good morning messages, nightly calls, knowing her favorite wine, songs, touch—felt perfect. She almost forgot his wife. But his questions became accusations: "Where were you last night?" "Why didn't you answer?" "Who were you with?"

Paola answered, hiding nothing, her French friend—loyal, more friend than lover—kept her grounded. She wasn't in love, but she kept him. Luca couldn't stand it.

"Leave him," he urged, tangled in bed.

"You don't need him. I'm here."

"You're married, why do you care?" Paola countered.

"Not for long," he claimed. "I've spoken to a lawyer. I'm leaving her." His words hit hard. She sat up, heart pounding.

"Would you really?"

He took her hand, eyes dangerously sincere.

"I've never felt this way. With you, I'm free, myself."

She trusted him. Bit by bit, she revealed her childhood, her fears, her dreams—letting herself cry once while he held her close. Luca responded to her questions, though never completely, unfamiliar with such vulnerability. He called her late, wanting to know where she was, even for the smallest, most ordinary things.

One evening, her dinner plans with friends prompted Luca's uninvited arrival. With a female friend, his clenched smile chilled the air.

"I didn't know you were so busy," said Luca.

"Why are you jealous?" Paola asked.

"Because you matter," he said.

It felt like control, not care—another warning sign she resisted. Luca, used to getting his way, obsessed over her.

She didn't want a cage, even a golden one with silk sheets, whispered promises. Yet when he said, "You're mine," she ached for it. Was this love or control? She couldn't tell—her father had controlled her too, and she knew, in his own way, he had loved her.

To prove she mattered, he invited her to the upscale Grand Hotel by Lake Maggiore. After checking in, hungry, they visited the restaurant, nearly empty save a solitary figure in ABBA-style silk, flawless makeup, eyes fixed on the door, waiting for someone absent.

They enjoyed dinner. A young woman approached hesitantly, her date absent, asking to join. The place was expensive, a refuge for the strange, wealthy, where appearances meant everything, nothing. Paola glanced at Luca, unsure. He nodded, smiling faintly. The evening shifted, charged with unpredictability, silent questions unvoiced.

The woman introduced herself: "I'm Monica, waiting for a friend," confident yet warm, discussing her work managing complex projects. Her words were steady, practiced.

"The restaurant's about to close, and I'm alone," she said hesitantly. "Mind if I come upstairs to finish my wine? It's no fun drinking alone."

Paola exchanged a glance with Luca, who nodded. "OK," Paola replied, gesturing to the seat. Monica brightened, slipping into their circle. The atmosphere shifted as they relaxed. She grabbed the bottle and followed them to their room. Paola and Luca sat on the bed, Monica on a chair, pouring wine. Silence stretched, conversation drying. Tension thickened.

Monica broke it, her voice low, tentative. "Would you... Mind if I watch you two?" Paola and Luca exchanged a hesitant look. She smiled, calm and polite. "I would mind."

Monica nodded, left quietly.

When Monica left, Paola spoke softly. "What did she want?"
Luca smiled lightly. "I don't know... imagine what she'd see if she stayed." He pulled Paola onto the bed, and they made love passionately. Sunlight spilled across their suite's terrace as they finished breakfast. Refreshed and curious, they decided to explore the hotel spa. The pool glistened under the midday sun, surrounded by lush gardens and sleek architecture. They received shoes—men in bright pink slippers, women in glossy black—a quirky touch. They luxuriated in steam rooms, calming pools. But the atmosphere felt charged, unexpected.
Couples, groups mingled openly, many same-sex pairs—a sanctuary wrapped in luxury. In the changing room, a man's subtle smile, a gentle touch sparked playful conversation, leaving Luca intrigued, unsettled. By the pool, a woman's knowing smile invited Paola, fluttering her heart with confusion. Leaving, they exchanged glances.
"This place," Paola said quietly, "is more than a spa."
Luca nodded. "Feels like a spot for LGBTQ dating, maybe?"
They left, understanding the hotel's subtle network of hidden interactions, private exchanges. The peculiar man at the bar made sense. They noticed more: men carrying women's bags, dressed expensively; women in designer clothing, expressions weary. Gestures hinted at unspoken routines, connections. They shared wealth, lust, exhaustion, and living double lives. Paola watched with quiet sadness—chasing desires, running on empty, eyes heavy beneath glamour. Luca, drawn in, pulse quickening, felt the restless energy spark something wild within.

Chapter 14:

The Plan

When Luca returned home, he sat at the table, thoughts running wild. His mind buzzed. How could he tell Paola that he'd soon be spending more time with his wife, who was about to give birth? He knew his life would flip upside down. He'd be a father, a husband—everything she needed. He couldn't lose the last solid ground beneath his feet, even if marriage were a cage. Paola's laughter, her passion—something rare he couldn't let go.

He didn't want to lose her, but he couldn't be fully hers either. He needed a solution—and found one. He'd rent an apartment in Rome: a quiet, safe place, far from his wife's prying eyes, where they could meet whenever he wanted, a secret, untraceable. He pictured a luxurious apartment in Prati, a sanctuary of calm. His wife wouldn't notice. Lies were ready, the plan set. He planned the game, but didn't know that Patrizia knew everything. She always knew—the other women, the late nights, the perfume not hers. She never exploded, didn't accuse, but balanced the scales her way. Her lover wasn't chosen for passion, but for power. Every move she made was a calculated play for control. She aimed to keep Luca under watch while living her own life with a lover he didn't suspect.

But Luca was distracted, thinking about Paola. If he wanted her to stay close, he had to offer more than just meetings—purpose, a reason to stay: work, independence, a high-class life in Rome. It was what she wanted. He called well-known designers, project managers he knew.

"Paola's talented, smart, hardworking," he told them. "She needs a chance to shine." After weeks of negotiations, offers rolled in. Paola landed modeling gigs, campaigns, runway shows—steady work, all based in Rome. From casting calls to job interviews, fashion shoots to potential movie roles, Rome offered everything to grow her career. Moving there wasn't just an option; it was the gateway to opportunities her talent deserved. With work's flexibility and a chance to build her reputation in fashion's heart, her decision became clear: Rome was where her future began.

Confused by the sudden Rome-centric opportunities, she sought Luca's guidance to make sense of it, hoping for advice.

"Rome has plenty of opportunities," Luca said one evening at a cozy bar, after a long day, when she raised the topic. "I want you to feel strong, independent, but know this: I'm here for you."

Paola wanted to trust him, even though her intuition whispered otherwise. She had stepped into a new chapter: fulfilling work, connections that opened doors. Luca had helped her become more than a secret lover. She could finally live fully, maybe even imagine a life with him.

But she ignored one thing: he was still tied to Patrizia—emotionally, financially, and mentally. Sometimes, he would watch her as if measuring her against someone else—and her intuition was right. He found himself comparing her to Patrizia, and even to his mother. He filtered her behaviors through his past, convinced she was acting for the same reasons. In doing so, he saw only what he feared to see—and the thought that she might be the same as them shook him. He hesitated. On one hand, he wanted a real relationship with Paola. On the other, he couldn't build one while still bound to his wife and while constantly comparing her to the others. He tried to understand why he was doing it. The only explanation he could find was that he kept measuring her value, comparing her not to others in general, but to the standards of wealth and the shadow of his mother. Whenever he erred, he responded with grandiose gestures rather than genuine apologies or any real self-reflection. And now he felt like the one truly messing up, so he created another grand gesture. It was meant to buy him time—and to get exactly what he want

Chapter 15:

Surprise

Everything went as Luca had planned. Paola was captivated, her curiosity, excitement, and ambition quietly entwined. He took the next step: renting a stylish Campo Marzio loft with a terrace and a city view.

"It's ours," he said, placing the keys in her hand.

"No one else. Just us."

Paola stepped inside, her breath quickening. Her fingers brushed smooth surfaces, as if touch could confirm the surrounding perfection. Every corner radiated sophistication, yet that perfection stirred a strange, incomprehensible unease. How could a space be so flawless, so meticulously designed, it felt unreal? Her eyes drifted to the terrace. Rome's terracotta rooftops glowed in the afternoon sun; the city's hum hushed in respect for the loft's quiet majesty. Yet, amid this calm, something whispered a warning.

The apartment was more than a home—a world crafted to enchant, seduce. Every detail, material, and the light's shadow was intentional, hiding secrets she'd yet to uncover.

The open-plan space amazed: clean architectural lines, soft gray tones, Italian marble gleaming in sunlight through floor-to-ceiling windows. A custom fireplace flickered, its dark stone, brushed brass framing plush furniture where time could pause.

The kitchen, a minimalist masterpiece—matte cabinetry, handleless doors, integrated appliances. A Carrara marble island stood like a sculpture under pendant lights, ready for food and wine rituals. The terrace, the true jewel, revealed a private oasis via sliding glass doors. A sunken Jacuzzi bubbled in one corner, dark stone edges soaking in the sun's last rays. A nearby outdoor fireplace burned, surrounded by oversized loungers and soft blankets for summer evenings. Lavender drifted from planters; under a modern pergola, a dining table for six awaited unforgettable nights.

The loft whispered luxury—not flashy, but confident, restrained, refined. A place seducing with quiet perfection. Paola stood at the window, eyes on the rooftops, feeling awe, a hint of fear. This wasn't just a sanctuary—it was a trap. Luca brought her here to bind her to his world, feeling like freedom. When they sat, he surprised her.

"I booked a hotel on the Amalfi Coast. We leave tomorrow."

"Just us," he said, voice low, eyes unreadable.

She closed her eyes, breathing, feeling. Rome wasn't just a city—it was a stage. Tonight, she was both audience and performer, balancing freedom and entrapment. She agreed, though something hesitated. His "tomorrow" felt like a gift, undeniable.

She glanced at Luca, his expression unreadable—charm, calculation. She'd felt it before, but tonight, in this luxurious world, it was undeniable. Wine rested on the marble island. Paola sipped, savoring the sharp sweetness, steadying her racing thoughts. I'm not naive, she thought, but maybe this is my chance. Rome stretched before her, promising adventure, danger. Stepping into this world would change everything.

Why now? she wondered.

Why so many opportunities, attention, here?

The loft felt like a reward to both. The Jacuzzi bubbled, lavender mingling with warm air, intoxicating, surreal. Paola felt awe, desire, and caution swirl like city lights below. That night, she gave him everything—trust, desire, hidden heart pieces. Every laugh, glance, touch laid her soul bare. And Luca realized something: if he told her what she wanted to hear, perhaps she wouldn't question him. All he had to do was give her what she desired, promise what she longed for, speak the words she wanted to hear. Perhaps that would be enough for her not to see whether everything truly aligned—and he could stretch his advantage for a while longer. Luca's intentions were conflicted. He wanted Paola, but he was still tied to his wife, and he wasn't ready to build a life with her yet. So, he mastered the art of appeasement: saying what she wanted to hear, promising what she yearned for, all the while keeping his real intentions hidden and stretching his advantage over time.

Morning light held its intensity like a presence. The apartment, alive with passion, hummed with its memory. Paola felt it in her bones—closeness, surrender, Luca's gaze. They'd depart soon, but the loft's elegance, secrets, and allure left its mark.

Arriving in Amalfi felt like a postcard. The hotel, carved into a cliffside, with balconies spilling over the sea like secrets. In their suite, pale limestone floors met linen sheets soft as skin, while the ocean stretched infinitely beyond the windows. Orange blossoms scented the warm air, mingling with sea salt, something sweeter. They spoke little that hour. The view stole words. Paola sat barefoot on the terrace, Champagne in hand, hair catching the golden light. Luca stood behind, silent, his hand on her shoulder, as if deciding if this was real. Beautiful, temporary, like the best things.

That night, after dinner, they sat in the piano bar's velvet glow. Soft jazz wove through clinking glasses, guest murmurs. Luca leaned in, kissed her neck slowly, willing time to stop, then whispered, "I have to run to the room—five minutes, I'll be back, I promise."

Paola nodded, dizzy from wine, skin tingling. She watched him vanish up marble stairs, into shadows, golden light. Finishing her drink at the bar, a woman entered—elegant, deliberate, curated beauty. She scanned the room, eyes landing on Paola. No smile, no politeness—just a steady stare, heavy with history, unfinished business, as if Paola trespassed. Paola didn't flinch. She kept her eyes down, scrolling her phone with practiced indifference. Her fingers slowed, the screen a haze beneath them. Moments stretched. Quiet steps approached. Paola started smiling, expecting Luca's voice, hand.

It wasn't him.

A woman—smooth, feline, too casual. Paola looked up. Her face was flawless, cold beauty for power, not warmth. Her eyes held Paola's, unapologetic. Everything quieted. Tall, raven-black hair, blood-red lips, she sat as if she belonged.

"I'm Alessia," she said softly. "May I sit? I'm alone, as you are."

Paola blinked. "No, I'm waiting for my boyfriend."

Something clicked, a faint unease flickering.

Luca planned it, though she didn't know. Every moment was prepared, but to Paola, it felt like a chance. Luca returned, smiling, unaware her intuition whispered more. Paola introduced Alessia. He ordered more Champagne. Alessia spoke of her room, inviting them. Luca let Paola decide. She said yes, not from curiosity, but because she had long viewed him through the lens of her father. Deep down, she was still that little girl, afraid of anger and eager to avoid it. Alessia's movements were slow, feline, deliberate, quickening Paola's pulse. Beautiful, magnetic, too confident.

Paola felt detached, suspended between disbelief and a darker intrigue she didn't name.

"I'm not here to pressure you," Alessia said.

Paola glanced at the door. Luca was in the bathroom. Alessia stood, removed her blouse, bare, unashamed. Paola pulled back, breath quickening, skin buzzing under Alessia's touch.

From the doorway, Luca's voice, low, smooth: "Kiss her. On her nipples. I want to see you lose control." He leaned against the doorframe, watching. It wasn't about Alessia—it was about Paola's reaction, hesitation, heat in her cheeks. Torn between revulsion and thrill, she hated how he made her question herself, how he affected her. To prove she was wild, unpredictable, she kissed Alessia—softly, briefly—then pulled away.

Luca drew in a sharp breath, confronted with everything he desired.

"This is your fantasy," she remarked.

"Not mine," Paola answered, collecting her things and walking away without a backward glance.

.

Luca trailed behind, each step deliberate, cautious.

"You think this is love?" Paola hissed.

"I thought you'd like it. You are wild and curious." Luca said, calm, calculated.

Her silence roared. He stepped closer.

"I want you. All of you. I'm divorcing Patrizia. I got us the apartment. What else should I do?"

"Stop trying to own me," Paola whispered.

"Stop pretending this is love when it's a game." The air crackled. Luca didn't argue, stepped closer.

"I love you, Paola," he said quietly. "I care for you. I want you to be free. I thought it would turn you on, give you something unforgettable."

She turned away, jaw clenched, adrenaline buzzing. Her mind screamed run, but his voice caught her.

"You didn't touch me," she said bitterly.

"You wanted to watch us."

"I wanted you happy, to see what you hide. I thought I gave you space." He reached for her wrist. She let him.

"You don't have to forgive me," he said.

"Don't shut me out. I'm trying, Paola. I don't know how to do this perfectly. I want you."

She saw something raw, maybe fear, in his eyes. Despite everything, chemistry weakened her walls.

"Why do I keep letting you in?" she murmured.

"Because this is real," he said. "Even when it hurts."

He kissed her—hungry, desperate, worshipping her mouth like salvation. They didn't speak again. Their bodies collided—wild, consuming, tangled in sheets, half-truths. No Alessia, no wife, no past, no rules. Only them, the unsaid.

After waking, unease lingered. She tested him.

At breakfast, she said, calm, deliberate, "I want to try something new." Luca's eyes flicked to hers, surprise masked by a cool smile.

"What do you mean?"

"A swinger club," she said evenly.

"Near Rome, a villa by the lake. They say it's elegant... and it's a place for people like us."

He paused, weighing her words, then nodded. "If that's what you want."

Paola held his gaze, steady. "I do. Let's go—tomorrow's Saturday."

He gave a small nod, consent quiet, complete.

Chapter 16:

Swinger Club

When it was meant to be fun, Luca was unusually proactive. He went online, quickly finding the elegant villa near Rome. At the swinger villa, they saw guests walking and lounging naked by the pool. Some held champagne, others engaged in sex. The reception was shrouded in shadows, velvet: black floors, purple-tinted walls, scents of amber, roses, and something primal—perhaps desire's memory. Guests, in their thirties and forties, radiated Italian charm and mystery. Laughter floated, controlled. Luca reserved a private room. As night fell, soft purple lights pulsed in the garden. In the large room, a sexy female DJ played a slow, charged mix of electro and minimal house. People moved as if they belonged—hugging, laughing, sipping dark drinks from crystal glasses. They sat in Turkish-themed costumes for dinner, voices low, intimate. Everyone seemed like lifelong friends, or pretended to be for the night. Paola and Luca wore no costumes; no one minded. Paola's black dress clung like a second skin. Luca, impeccable, barely spoke to others. She noticed: he was distant, polite but cold, as if performing for her. That excited her briefly—he was hers. Though all eyes were on them, Luca's were on her. After dinner, Paola followed Luca, fingers gliding along black velvet walls. She didn't ask questions—this place held no answers.

The space unfolded: curtained lounges, open doors, rooms bathed in artificial light. Beds everywhere—some occupied, others waiting, veiled by darkness, blurring identity, not intention. Paola paused in their room. Inside, walls breathed quiet music, bedding turned down, a single wine glass by the bed. Luca's half-smile suggested he knew what she feared, what she wanted. The air held incense, wine, and something unmistakable. Upstairs, guest rooms glowed with half-light and half-shadow.

Beds, large and inviting, stood like altars in a temple of temptation. Soft lighting, almost too dim, gave a dreamlike quality. Whispers drifted behind thin curtains, shadows moving like gossip. A place without shame—a theater of curiosity, control, surrender, and indulgence. Yet beneath the surface, power flowed like whispered desire, masks fell with quiet seduction, and new ones emerged, promising even darker pleasures.

Paola followed Luca down the corridor, sensing the answers. His gaze shifted—not just desire, but curiosity, waiting to see if she'd follow through. As midnight neared, guests undressed, paired off, and vanished into beds. A woman with blonde hair touched Paola's shoulder.

"You're beautiful," she said. "Join us?" The man beside her smiled warmly, respectfully.

Paola looked at Luca. He nodded slightly, almost imperceptibly. Suddenly, it wasn't her game. She followed the couple upstairs, Luca behind, his hand on her back. The room, softly lit, held cushions and candles. The woman unzipped

Paola's dress with practiced ease, her touch gentle, skilled. But when her hands slid lower, Paola froze. Her body screamed no—not from the woman, but from emptiness. Curiosity faded; she was tired. She pulled away gently.

"I'm sorry, I can't," Paola said quietly.

"It's okay," the woman answered and smiled kindly.

Paola dressed, her hands trembling.

"I thought you wanted this," Luca said.

"I did," she replied. "Until now." They stood in silence.

Silence stretched between them, thick and suffocating. He couldn't understand why she had pulled back, and she couldn't understand why he seemed unable—or unwilling—to accept it. Every unspoken thought, every withheld feeling, pulsed between them like an electric current.

That night, sleep eluded them—blaring music and restless neighbors filling the apartment. They reached for each other, but the unspoken misunderstanding held them at a distance.

Sunlight streamed through the sheer curtains, draping the terrace in warmth. Paola leaned close at breakfast, her lips near Luca's ear, her words a teasing caress. He stayed silent at first, tired and distracted, yet a subtle tension ran between them, pulling them together even as hesitation held them apart. Her touch under the table spoke wordlessly. His eyes darkened; without a word, he took her hand, leading her upstairs. Later, by the pool, the scene grew bolder, freer. More guests arrived; laughter echoed through palms, naked bodies glistened, unabashed. Luca, relaxed, perhaps too much, slipped off Paola's swimsuit in the water, wanting to penetrate her. She didn't want to, trying to laugh it off. Unsure about exposure among strangers' lingering gazes, she hesitated. Luca didn't ask, didn't wait, loving her as he wanted. When it ended, they dressed quietly and returned to Rome. The apartment felt colder. They both knew something was wrong. Luca felt compelled to leave—not only because his wife was about to give birth, but because he couldn't face the conflict between them. Like a child overwhelmed by anger or fear, he fled, believing distance could dissolve the discomfort. By morning, he was on a plane— *"business meetings,"* he lied—blind to the reality of his wife's impending labor.

Chapter 17:

Birth

While Luca flew to Milan, Paola remained in Rome, immersing herself in work. Not for financial gain, but to rediscover the woman she had been before Luca. The camera, the elegant clothes, her ambition—they reminded her that she had value far beyond his world.

Meanwhile, Luca buried himself in work, as if their silence wasn't distance but routine. They drifted apart without admitting it—two satellites caught in each other's pull, spinning on opposite orbits. They promised to meet soon, but neither knew when. Days passed, and she wrote that she was going to Milan.

He hesitated, then wrote: "I'm really sorry, but I can't meet you in Milan now, it's too risky." As Luca texted Paola, cries echoed from the delivery room. His parents had arrived at the hospital. Pressure rose, sharp and unrelenting, as if he stood on a knife's edge.

His mother's gaze bore into him, stern and unwavering. His father masked his disappointment, but it slipped through.

"Be strong," he said quietly. "We expect a great father." Luca couldn't reply to Paola now; it was impossible. She noticed his nervousness, assuming it was just a tough day, a business problem, and wrote: "It looks like your life is trapped." Luca sighed, eyes narrowing. "I'm torn," he admitted. "Work, family, you're far—everything's falling apart in my hands."

As his wife's pains intensified, her screams filled the air. Luca apologized, promised to reply later, and put the phone down. Trapped amid a family expecting strength, his heart broke inside. Paola knew she had to be patient. "We're in this together," she wrote, whispering to herself, "whatever that means."

The sterile hospital room was thick with tension. Luca stood by the window, face pale and drawn. Outside, the city moved, unaware; inside, everything changed forever. His wife's cries faded into exhaustion. Then—a newborn's sharp wail pierced the silence. A nurse gently brought the baby girl to Luca. Tiny, fragile, with dark eyes that seemed to hold the weight of the world, her skin soft and perfect, her hands curled into delicate fists. She was beautiful—impossibly so. But Luca didn't see beauty. A cold wave of dread swept through him. His throat tightened.

His heart pounded—not with joy, but fear and confusion. The child in his arms accused everything he'd tried to escape. Responsibility crashed over him like a tidal wave. The future, freedom—shattered. This tiny life demanded what he wasn't ready to give. His hands shook as he gazed at her innocent, helpless face. He hated his betraying emotions.

How could he feel this way about his daughter? A desperate urge surged—a need to flee, to escape fatherhood's suffocating chains. To disappear from the hospital, from the birth, from the new life. To run from a responsibility that felt like a prison. His wife's soft voice whispered, "She's ours. We must be strong." Luca couldn't answer. His mind raced, torn between duty and panic. Every instinct screamed to walk out, leave it all behind, find a place where he wasn't a father. For a long moment, he wanted to vanish.

So, he texted Paola: "I need you. Come to Tuscany. Just us. No eyes. No pressure. I'll send a driver." She read it twice, then agreed.

Chapter 18:

Couple in Tuscany

The Tuscan villa sat high on a hill, wrapped in silence and sunlight. No signs, no neighbors—just land stretching far, golden, endless. Then, it appeared: a stone house, half-buried in wild lavender and rosemary, hidden like a secret waiting to be kept. Beautiful, but not postcard-perfect. The air inside was heavy, something unspoken. Shutters ajar, as if the house were watching. Walls soaked with whispered stories: late arrivals, silence over wine, touches that meant something, then claimed. The pool overlooked hills, greenery melting into blue haze.

Cypress trees stood as silent guards at the garden's edge; olive trees twisted, telling old tales. A distant tower bell chimed slowly, melancholically. The garden, vast, untrimmed, deliberately wild—as if someone had tried taming it, then let it grow free.

Hidden corners, benches under fig trees, a stone table for midnight dinners. Inside, the house stayed cool despite the heat. Arched doors led to rooms of shadows and sunbeams; thick walls held the scent of wood smoke. The bedroom's fireplace, unused for months, linens crisp, windows tall. Every detail chosen—yet kept at a distance.

When Paola arrived, Luca was there, greeting her with light, practiced kisses on each cheek, as if they'd never tangled in breath. He poured wine without asking.

"Isn't it perfect?" he smiled. Paola nodded.

It was. But it felt like a place for pretending, and she'd had enough. The host, in the kitchen, handed her wine with a long look, no words.

"I hope you don't mind," he said. "Another couple's coming. Last-minute. Friends of friends."

Paola's throat tightened.

"Is that okay?" Luca asked, knowing her answer wouldn't change anything. She nodded. "Sure." But she was unsettled, wanting to be alone with Luca, to understand him. Waiting frustrated her. The couple arrived: she, barely twenty-five, with a delicate, uncertain smile, a scar down her face—noticed, then ignored. He, older, bald, with too many white teeth misaligned for his age. He was drawn to Paola, his hand sliding down her back as he sat on her right. Paola shivered.

"Don't," she said firmly.

He laughed, as if it were a game. "Come on, we're friends. Wine?"

Paola's eyes burned at Luca, on her left. "What is this?"

"It's a place to explore. You wanted freedom," Luca said.

"I wanted to be me. Not a toy. Not merchandise."

The man watched her like prey. His girl, quiet, looked at Luca, awaiting permission to speak, standing nearby. Something in Paola broke. She grabbed her coat and left. The man's laughter followed. Outside, cold air woke her. Luca followed, voice low, pleading.

"What are you doing, Luca? Inviting people like that into our space, acting unaware?"

"I thought you'd like something different," Luca said.

"Different?" Paola laughed bitterly. "You wanted to see how far I'd break."

He didn't answer.

"Do you know who you are?" Paola asked again.

He blinked. "No," he said quietly, meaning it.

The villa was silent; the couple gone. Luca sat by the fireplace, dressed, staring at the flames for answers. What are you doing, Luca? He'd built a charming, successful, dangerous, safe self that women wanted. It always worked—except with Paola. With her, he felt real: drunk laughter, her hand in his shirt, her gaze seeing behind his mask. That scared him. His wife hadn't touched him since pregnancy; they were strangers. Manipulator? Sometimes. Coward, liar? Yes. He hated it. At the warped mirror, he saw a man playing God with emotions he didn't understand, afraid to be seen. Paola's words echoed: "Do you know who you are?" No. Time to find out. He deleted escort apps, secret messages. No call to his wife—truth later. He opened a blank notebook, writing: Who are you alone? What do you want beyond sex? What's love and honesty? Paola's footsteps crunched on gravel. He stayed, writing, facing what he'd avoided, waiting as she slipped into bed.

In the morning, Luca made espresso, stood on the stone balcony, feigning calm. Inside, he spun. Change was hard. Words failed him—deals, yes; emotions, no. He knew touch, bodies speaking. By afternoon, he said, "Come with me." She followed, not warmly, but curiously, hair up, sunglasses on, controlling. He saw through it—she was measuring him.

Silently, he led her upstairs, stripped her ritually, kissed her like therapy, and touched her as if confessing. It worked, briefly. That night, awake beside her, he was haunted—not by her, but by unadmitted thoughts: a man with high cheekbones, a transgender woman in a sheer dress. Her elegance stirred something raw. He hadn't told Paola. How could he? No words for himself. Not "gay," just searching. Maybe pleasure was misdirection. Maybe he wanted to understand his hunger. Confused, ego-driven, he opened his laptop, typed privately: "Trans girl Milan." "First gay experience confession." "Can straight men like men?" Ridiculous, juvenile, electric. He felt sixteen, alive, and afraid. Would Paola judge? Leave? Understand? She was wild, creative. Maybe she'd stay. He closed the laptop, looked at her sleeping, wanting to keep her, to say: "I'm lost. I don't know what I am. I'm scared I like things I shouldn't."

Can you want me? But he didn't say it. He held her, hoping she'd feel his truth. When Paola woke, she sat on the bed's edge, silent, her legs draped in the sheet, eyes fixed on the distance.

"Do you ever feel," she whispered, "that what hurts you makes you alive?" Luca watched, not with desire, but understanding.

"I think," she continued, eyes distant, "I didn't realize I enjoyed pain until you spanked me. Not for pain, but because it reminded me of my past."

He moved closer.

"My mother," she said, "was very dominant. I couldn't speak freely; she'd get angry, distant, draining me with control, punishing with silence, judgments, threats, words.

She claimed love when I was good. My father, strict, yelling, never listened, and sometimes hit, spanked me. Mother said they loved me, but I had to be good, not resist. I grew up thinking love is conditional, pain is love, discomfort is notice." Paola craved love, hurting in her chest, hands, and voice. But when love neared, she stiffened, scared, starting arguments, pulling away, testing if they'd chase. She pushed them away, expecting disappointment, breaking what she needed. She knew why. True love—quiet, steady—was foreign, dangerous, not matching her chaos. Her instincts didn't trust it. Love hurt, left if you weren't perfect, punished flaws. Soft, real love? She didn't know how to handle it, so she sabotaged, controlling rejection. She confused love with danger, attracting men like Luca, who disappointed, as expected. Wounded people build shields, call it independence.

That day, by the villa's window, sunbathing olive groves, something opened—not heartbreak, but understanding. She was tired of running, destroying, and confusing love with fire. Maybe she wasn't broken, just afraid. Luca sat beside her, understanding.

"My mom wanted a son in suits, marrying an educated girl," he said. "They paid for business school, set the map—what a man should be. I hated it, did the opposite. Taboo felt mine, even if senseless."

He paused. "Mom still controls me, wants me close, I am not her husband. I can't explain her—she wouldn't understand. I keep a distance. Everyone wants something, but can I be there for myself?"

"Like now," she said. He nodded. Her eyes shone with a question.

"You want something again, right?"

He hesitated.

"An idea," he said, "to try something. With someone else. With you."

Paola wasn't scared; she expected his unpredictability.

"A transgender woman," he said. "I want to see what it's like. With you. If you suggested it, maybe it wouldn't be strange."

She stared. "You want me to ask, so you don't admit you want it, feel ashamed?"

His silence answered. She touched his hand.

"I don't know if I want it," she said. "But I want to understand why you do. That's more real than avoiding our truth."

Luca looked down, no fantasy to hide in, just confusion. "I feel like a stranger," he said. "Even to myself."

"I've been a stranger my life," she whispered. "That's why I let men hurt me. To feel something."

"What now?" he asked.

She pressed her forehead to his.

"We stop pretending we're just wild," she said.

"We admit we're hurt. Decide to heal or keep running. Maybe you're not a patch for my wounds, but maybe being together's enough."

Luca met her eyes, no hesitation, just resolve.

"I don't know the future," he said softly. "But I want you in it. Maybe we can visit nice places." Paola smiled faintly.

"A holiday?" He nodded.

"Somewhere new, quiet, just us."

He took and kissed her hand. "I'll take you soon."

"I need a couple of weeks to fix something," Luca added.

Paola squeezed his hand, feeling trust, hope. She didn't ask what he needed to fix; silence spoke for them. They lay in bed, dreaming of a future that didn't have to hurt.

Chapter 19:

The Baby is born

While his wife returned to work, Luca stayed home. It wasn't punishment. For the first time, he had a reason to stop, truly pay attention to someone without expectations—someone who breathed, smiled, and relied on him.

When the baby arrived, everything else lost weight. Work, meetings, goals—once life's purpose—faded. He did what he'd once seen as a weakness: disconnected from the business world. Each morning, he woke before the baby, watching her sleeping face. Something sacred lay in it—stillness, subtle lip movements, faint breathing. When she woke, smiling effortlessly, Luca felt the universe affirm his existence. He gave bottles, changed diapers, played guitar, and sang.

He learned her rhythms—when she needed closeness, quiet, holding, or just his presence. It was love he'd never known—quiet, pure, unconditional. He often thought of Paola—her laughter, touch, their deep conversations. He wished she were here. But sadness dissolved when the baby's hand touched his cheek, as if saying, "You're needed here. You're loved."

When his wife came home, the atmosphere thickened. Tired, irritable, withdrawn, she hated her post-birth body, herself. Luca couldn't fix that. His words about the baby stung her.

"So, you're mother of the year now?" she snapped once, after he mentioned the baby holding her head up that day.

"No, I spent the day with her," he replied gently.

"Yeah? Congratulations. An emotional tourist picking parts that move him."

He fell silent, lacking energy to argue, not wanting to. It wasn't about fighting, but her inner pain. Day by day, the wall between them grew. She did what she wanted—late nights with "friends," ignoring his calls, never asking about his day with the baby.

At work, she belittled him. "Luca? He's on paternity leave," she'd say, smirking. "Finally, someone who doesn't talk back." People laughed. Yet each evening, as the baby slept in his arms, tenderness returned, certainty too. This was real, not illusion or escape. This was home. He lived in two worlds: one with the baby, love simple, direct, and maskless; one with his wife, who no longer knew herself, let alone him. Something stirred—a desire to return to his old world, not as escape, but as a reunion with a self he needn't deny as a father.

One night, he spoke cautiously to his wife. She didn't look at him. "That's unnecessary," she said quietly. "The company's fine. Everything's smooth."

"I know, but I want to be part of it. The company's like my second child."

Her silence startled him, as if she'd decided without him. The next morning, he wore a shirt unworn for months, went to the office, his former kingdom. The elevator, hallway, and glass doors looked the same, but not like home. In the boardroom, no one stood, no one welcomed him—just awkward silence. His assistant was gone, his seat taken by an unknown office manager. He tried to engage, suggest improvements, rocking the stroller. He spoke of restructuring, efficiency. No one responded. A team lead exchanged a look with a colleague, smirked.

He felt like a prop, a dad on paternity leave "playing CEO." He shut himself in his office, called his lawyer, needing confirmation of a fear unspoken.

"Yes, Luca," the lawyer said carefully. "Your wife transferred the company into a trust. Legally, you're not the owner. In practice, it's not yours." Silence lingered. His breathing echoed. The silence wasn't deafening—hollow, empty. Betrayal not in one act, but slow exile.

He'd lost what he'd built. Not through war or collapse, but because he believed fatherhood meant giving fully. Instead of gratitude, he found isolation—from his wife, work, and himself. That evening, Luca wrote to his wife: "You wanted the child. Now you care for her. I'm leaving—for a holiday. I need to remember who I am."

He packed a small suitcase—shirts, a notebook, and an unfinished novel. Leaving the baby sleeping, his heart broke, but he couldn't stay. He kissed her forehead, whispered, "I'll return when I know how." He walked away.

Chapter 20:

Under the skin

When Luca arrived in Rome, evening had settled over the city. Paola waited, as he'd asked. He'd said he needed a drink, but they both knew it was more. The hotel bar was dim, lit like a forgotten film scene. Jazz drifted through velvet air; Paola swirled her wine, watching Luca check his phone, fearing his wife.

"You're nervous," she said.

"No, just... excited." He answered too quickly.

"About what?"

He glanced at the door.

Then she walked in—tall, striking, confident, in a black satin dress that clung like liquid. Her eyes scanned, landing on Luca. She approached without hesitation.

"Hi, may I sit? I'm alone," she said, her voice shimmering between masculine and feminine.

"Sure, join us," Luca said.

"Luca?" Paola looked, confused. "You know her?"

"We don't," he said, standing awkwardly. Gina smiled, her presence like perfume. Paola nodded stiffly. Something felt off, but she didn't want to seem jealous, not after promising openness. When Gina ordered nothing, touching Luca only when Paola wasn't looking, her stomach twisted. Feeling foolish, Paola wanted to flee to their room.

Inside, she asked quietly, "Who is she, really?"

"Just someone who likes people like us," Luca said, avoiding her gaze.

"Adventurous."

"Can I invite her up? To talk, explore?"

Paola agreed, curious. Gina entered in a silk robe, sensual, letting it fall away. When Luca moved toward her, his face changed—not lust, but hunger, deeper than for Paola, like seeking himself in Gina's body and beauty. Paola watched him kiss Gina's shoulder, chest. She didn't stop him yet, trying to understand. He looked at Paola.

"Come closer," he said.

"No," she whispered. "I don't want this."

"But you're curious."

"Jesus, Luca, you booked an escort without telling me? Used me to hide your secret?" she hissed.

"I thought you'd say no," he said.

"I needed to know, feel it, see if I was..."

"What?" she snapped.

"Gay? Bi? Whatever?"

"If I were me." He glanced at Gina, then Paola.

"I hope you find out," Paola said, grabbing her coat. "I won't be your experiment."

She left, bags in hand, leaving Luca with the stranger embodying what he couldn't be. But Luca followed her from the room. That night, Paola hadn't slept, hadn't cried—colder than sadness. Disappointment, detachment, like watching another's life, realizing it's hers. She saw Luca's eyes when Gina disrobed—that flicker, hunger, not for her, but internal, like drowning on purpose. Not angry, she felt curiosity. Why?

Why had Luca gone behind her again, booking an escort, lying, pulling her into a scene she didn't choose? Power? Punishment? Carelessness? Lost? Her hand shook, thoughts racing. Maybe he wasn't cruel, but lying to himself. Raised in suits, rules—Christian school, Catholic mother, a wife he couldn't leave—his life dictated, until sex, transgression, became freedom, truth.

Gina—tall, smooth-skinned, voice like dusk—wasn't just a woman, but a question, a boundary's riddle. Luca wanted to break every line he'd been told to stay within. Maybe that's why he wanted Paola—she could hurt or heal him, and he didn't care which, if he felt something. But now she saw him. He sought a mirror, not sex—someone to show who he was beneath the mask, money, marriage. Transgender women, perhaps, reflected his fluidity, secret, shame, and desire to be what he wasn't allowed to be. Where did that leave her? A prop? Permission slip? A woman confusing pain for love?

She closed her eyes, whispering, "I wasn't what he wanted—just a key to his door." Maybe he couldn't decide for himself, let alone for them. A man who chose, even badly, was stronger than one who couldn't. A confident man faced consequences, fixed mistakes. A man without confidence avoided conflict, feared himself, unaware of his strength.

Paola knew she had to step back; she couldn't risk Luca ruining her life. She withdrew subtly—slower replies, less urgent words, hours before answering, days filled with friends, not him. She needed space to breathe, think. Luca sensed it, responding with grand gestures.

Chapter 21:

Sardinian nights

The promise of a holiday, meant to mend or perhaps ensnare, had brought them to Sardinia's Costa Smeralda. The fire between Paola and Luca still burned, but for her, this was their final chance. They arrived at dawn, the sun gilding the jagged coastline as Luca navigated their rented Lamborghini along winding roads fringed with juniper and cork oak. Perched on granite cliffs, the iconic Hotel Cala di Volpe emerged, its pastel façade and bobbing boats heralding their arrival.

The lobby glowed with understated glamour: driftwood furnishings, coral-hued fabrics, and glass walls opening onto terraced pools. Sea salt and citrus scented the air. They were ushered to Suite 107, a lavish retreat with a private terrace, plunge pool, and sweeping views of Cala di Mezzo cove.

As dusk fell, they strolled arm in arm through fragrant gardens to the cliff-side restaurant. Lanterns flickered in the cooling breeze, waves crashing softly below. Their table overlooked sails and the horizon, a perfect backdrop for the unspoken tension between them.

They savoured fresh lobster risotto, grilled sea bream, and carpaccio, their glasses sparkling with crisp Vermentino di Gallura. After dinner, they retreated to their terrace, where stars stretched endlessly above. Their lips met in slow, reverent kisses, each touch a dialogue of longing and trust. Paola felt a connection deeper than any she'd known, even as she vowed to pull away. Every movement, every brush of skin, drew them closer—not just physically but emotionally. Luca's focus enveloped her, their shared space a fragile sanctuary. They held each other through the night, bodies and hearts entwined, until sleep claimed them, warm and unshakably close.

Morning bathed the terrace in sunlight and sea breeze. They lingered over breakfast—fresh figs, creamy ricotta, granita, and cappuccino—letting the Mediterranean's calm seep into their bones. Later, they boarded a sleek Riva yacht, slicing through turquoise waves. Paola dove into the water, laughing as sunlight kissed her hair, sparkling across the rippling sea. Luca watched, mesmerized, his heart lifting with her effortless joy. They anchored near Capriccioli, a hidden inlet rimmed with pink granite. Snorkeling masks on, they dove into cobalt waters, vibrant fish darting around ancient boulders. Back on deck, Paola draped herself across Luca's lap. His finger traced her curves, drawing a shiver until she melted against him. That evening, they wandered to the bar, nestled among pines overlooking the bay. Over Mirto, they shared hopes and regrets in the amber half-light. Paola spoke of her modelling career in Rome. Luca listened quietly, his gaze slipping inward, shadowed by thoughts of his wife and child. His distance stung. She wanted to follow him into that silence, to understand the ache she sensed. Sitting beside her, he was present yet absent, an absence that hurt more than words. His thoughts drifted to his family, torn between desire for Paola and the life he'd left behind. Guilt, fear, or doubt—something held him back, leaving him half-committed, a coward in his own heart.

Luca reached for his wallet to settle the bill, but his card was declined. He tried again, brow furrowing. No luck. A cold wave of panic crept up his spine. His phone buzzed at the front desk: a bank message. "Your card transactions have been temporarily blocked due to exceeded limits."

He called Paola to the terrace, away from curious eyes. "My card isn't working," he admitted, face flushed.

"I can't pay the hotel bill."

Paola frowned. "Did you forget to update your limits?"

He shook his head. "My wife lowered them. She's controlling the finances now. I had no idea until now." The luxurious holiday, the glittering nights—they were more fragile than he'd thought.

"I don't want to ruin this, but we need a plan."

Paola squeezed his hand.

"We'll find an apartment nearby for the rest of our stay."

Luca nodded, the weight of his situation settling in his chest.

"I hate feeling powerless."

Paola smiled softly. "Here, we have each other. That's what counts." They packed their bags and left the hotel behind. Paola found a stunning apartment—high ceilings, designer furniture, a rooftop pool overlooking the city skyline. The first night was perfect: bubbly in the hot tub, warm laughter, tender intimacy by the pool, reminiscent of their early days.

On the second afternoon, over wine, Luca said casually, "The owner offered a discount if we let two women stay here for one night. It's a huge place—five bedrooms. He'll give us cash back."

Paola blinked. "What do you mean, two women?"

"His friends, a couple, are visiting for one night. They'll be discreet."

"Luca..." Her voice carried a warning.

"They won't invade," he said. "I thought... maybe you'd be curious, like before."

She hesitated. Part of her wanted to refuse. Another part, still entangled with his desires, nodded. "Fine," she said.

The women arrived—tall, elegant, draped in black. Lana and Zoe's eyes lingered, their smiles too knowing. They shared the rooftop pool, talking of age, work, and interests. Luca poured drinks, music swelling, the air thick with expectation. One reached for Paola's hand. She didn't pull away—not at first.

Hours later, the four tangled on the massive bed, limbs and breath entwined. But something felt wrong. Paola felt detached, like she was watching herself perform. Lana's hands were soft, Zoe's mouth skilled, but it sparked no fire. She glanced at Luca, his gaze that of a director, not a lover. This wasn't her curiosity—it was his control. She excused herself, locked the bathroom door, and returned to a quieter room. The woman slipped away at dawn, leaving empty wine glasses and a forgotten scarf.

Luca stretched lazily in bed. "They weren't even that pretty in daylight, were they?"

Paola turned, voice flat. "I noticed everything."

He kissed her shoulder, oblivious. But something shifted in her chest—not desire, but clarity.

In the living room, Luca clutched his phone, jaw tight. His wife's voice was calm, unyielding, each word a reminder of the life beyond this room.

"Please, I need access to the money," he pleaded. "The limits are too low. I can't pay for anything."

A sigh on the other end.

"Luca, it's because of our child. You left her alone. That's unacceptable. I lowered the limits to protect her."

He gripped the phone tighter.

"What do you mean? You were home with her."

"It's more complicated," she said quietly. "I can't leave it to chance. Come home. We'll talk."

The call ended. Luca sat, heart heavy. Paola, overhearing, felt something break. This holiday was meant to be their last chance, not another lie.

She spoke softly. "She mentioned a child?" Luca nodded, eyes darkening. "Yes."

"We need to clear things up. No more secrets," she said, hand on his shoulder.

He exhaled. "Think what you want... I love you. I have a child. It isn't very easy. I didn't want to lie, but..."

Paola watched his pain, his relief.

"We have to get through this," he added.

She sat back, clarity sharpening.

It wasn't the child or the money—it was Luca's hiding, his refusal to be present, a pattern she'd ignored. No amount of talking could make him take responsibility. He was trapped in fear, seeing himself as the victim.

"I see it now," she said steadily. "This—us, the hiding, the blame, the fear—it's not something I can fix. You must face it yourself. I can't save you, Luca."

His anger flared, predictable and sharp, followed by silence. But Paola wouldn't stay. She couldn't. Staying meant confirming her pain, her broken heart. They changed their flight, returning to Rome. At her apartment, she met Luca's gaze.

"You need to leave now," she said, voice unwavering. This was about her, her space, her choice. She turned away, leaving him alone with his truth.

Luca never knew how to be alone. Solitude brought questions he suppressed: Who am I? Where am I going? What does this mean? Those thoughts pricked like thorns, preventing peace. He surrounded himself with chaos—people, noise, nights with Paola—to drown the inner voice. In her, he could be someone else: strong, in control. But in quiet, he was vulnerable, terrified of himself. Without overcoming that fear, he'd remain trapped, endlessly escaping instead of finding himself.

Chapter 22:

Return

Luca returned home, a battle awaiting him.

His wife stood in the doorway, her gaze sharp, as if she could read his every thought.

"So, you're back," she said coldly, letting him linger on the threshold like an unwelcome guest.

"We need to clear some things up," Luca began cautiously. She cut him off. "You? Clear things up?"

Her laugh was sharp, mocking. "You lack the strength to face your own problems."

Her sarcastic laughter drowned his words.

"You're like a bare butt on ice," she said, leaning closer, her voice dripping with disdain. "No control. And now, with a child, we've got you exactly where we want you."

Her words carried a newfound power, wielded like a mistress holding all the cards. Their discussion was over.

Luca scrambled to defend his weakening ground. Each day felt like a skirmish against an invisible foe. Her uncompromising stare met him the moment he stepped inside.

"Why's the kitchen a mess again? You can't even tell the cleaning lady what to do?" she snapped.

"Look at that sink," she added, leaving no room for excuses.

Luca lowered his eyes. "Sorry, I had a lot going on..."

"I'm tired of last-minute fixes. If you can't manage the maid, you'll clean it yourself," she said, her tone final.

Her relentless criticism drained his confidence, making him feel smaller with every word. He began to see she was stripping away not just his money but his dignity.

"The apartment smells," she pressed on.

Luca nodded, his voice faint. "I'll try..."

"Trying isn't enough. Act like an adult."

Her daily barbs, her angry eyes, her endless accusations chipped away at him. Helplessness grew, his efforts seeming futile.

He started to believe he was incapable and worthless. It was a punishment worse than any words. Then came her next blow.

"You know, I'm not exactly faithful either," she said, her tone icy.

"You think I'm here just for you? I'm playing my own game, and you're nowhere near understanding it."

Confusion and helplessness tightened Luca's throat. Her words were poison, seeping deep. It wasn't just infidelity—it was a toxic game dragging him under.

"There you have it," she said, turning away.

"This is reality. If you think you can change it, you're crazier than I thought."

Luca stood frozen, trapped in the darkness she'd painted. His wife was dismantling him, holding his life in her grip, every attempt at resistance ending in pain. To her, he was no longer a man but a frightened boy, cowering under life's weight, always defending, always fleeing.

In her eyes, it was simple: Luca's trembling during arguments, his apologies instead of action, marked him as incapable of responsibility, unable to protect himself or their family. Her harshness tested how much he could endure, each criticism a whip, each word a challenge to his fading strength.

But Luca took it as proof of his weakness. Instead of rising, he retreated further into himself, her words shattering him. The weight of betrayal crushed him, yet he saw no path but to endure. In their toxic dance, both were prisoners.

Chapter 23:

Luca's Women

Paola ignored Luca's calls and messages. Weeks passed, her silence absolute—messages read, calls unanswered, not even a curt demand to leave her alone. Luca hated silence more than anger. Anger meant he still mattered; silence closed the door for good. Alone in his apartment, the air too still, the windows too clear, he scrolled through old messages from Paola, thumb hovering over her name, as if staring could summon her. When that failed, his mind drifted to familiar escapes. Luca craved variety, seeing women like paintings in a gallery—each a story worth experiencing. Young, old, thin, curvy, dancers, actresses, art students, divorced mothers—he wanted them all.

Escorts held a unique allure. They asked no questions, demanded no change. With them, Luca could be unapologetic, asking for what he wanted without shame. No awkward silences, no hidden judgments. They offered everything, and he gave his full attention in return, relishing the control—the rules, the tone, the pace. It was a rhythm that felt safe. Tanya had been his anchor, giving without expectation. But now, even she didn't answer. He texted: "Hello, how are you? Are you okay?" No reply. Then: "I've been thinking about you. Want to

talk?" Nothing. He called. Voicemail. Tried again the next day.
Same result.

By the third day, he didn't know what he sought—comfort,
guilt, closure, or just a desperate need to matter. He emailed
her a dinner invitation, then a longer apology. Silence. He
remembered her faded green door, worn at the corners, brass
handle always cold. One gray afternoon, he went there,
planless, empty-handed, an ache in his stomach he couldn't
name. He rang once, twice, waiting. Nothing. Then a creak
nearby. An older woman emerged, wrapped in a knitted
sweater, her face etched with weary years. "Looking for her?"
she asked.

Luca faltered. "Tanya?"

"She's gone," the woman said, shaking her head.
"Found her two days ago in the bathtub. Pills, they say.
It was... sad. Not surprising."

Luca's mouth dried. "She... took her own life?"

The woman nodded. "She always seemed elsewhere, like she
didn't belong." The door closed.

Luca stood before the green door, motionless, something inside
him collapsing. It wasn't love, not like with Paola, but Tanya
had given him something raw, vital—a listener now lost. He
walked away, past trees whispering in the wind, silence trailing
him, now named: fear. He sought escape, not healing, craving
something gentle, quiet, where he could vanish. Typing "erotic
massage Rome" into a search engine, he expected a guilty fix.
Instead, a listing caught him: "Tantric Temple: Sensual

Awakening and Inner Presence." It sounded absurd, too spiritual, but a whisper urged: Try it.

He booked an appointment. The massage room glowed warm and golden, incense curling like a dream. The woman who greeted him wasn't seductive but calm, rooted, her eyes kind. She lit a candle and met his gaze. "Before we touch the body, we touch the soul."

Luca nearly laughed, but her presence stopped him. The ritual began with deep, slow breaths, his body a temple, not a tool. Her touch was unhurried, not to ignite desire but to awaken him. He dissolved—not sexually, but emotionally, spiritually. Waves rolled down his spine, through his chest, to his fingertips, a calm, encompassing pleasure, like being held by the universe. Tears welled as he lay there, unaware he could feel such purity, a pleasure that gave, restoring him to himself.

In that quiet, Paola flickered in his mind—not a conquest, but a flame. He imagined touching her without taking, offering safety, reverence. He pictured her body responding to a love that opens. Leaving the Tantric Temple, Luca felt lighter, transformed. He no longer craved conquest but connection. He didn't know if Paola would let him near again, but if she did, he vowed to show her a love

that began with breath. The tantric experience had torn down a wall, leaving his body, mistakes, and shame raw and real, like ash in his lungs. The energy of the women he'd used lingered, bruises under his skin.

Chapter 24:

The House Where Women Pay

Paola never imagined seeking solace this way, but she knew she couldn't surrender to the first man who might mask her pain. After Luca—after the silences, the betrayals—she stopped pretending love hadn't wounded her. She needed to piece together the fragments of herself. Booking the appointment under a false name, she found a website that promised "connection, attention, fantasy— for women who dare to choose themselves," never explicitly mentioning sex.

The villa, nestled in the hills outside Siena, was a sanctuary of stone walls and candlelit hallways, scented with roses and shadows. Each room bore a name, not a number. Alessio, her guide, asked her to choose one. He gave her time to refresh, knocking softly minutes later. No introductions, no questions—just a moment of stillness, the beginning of something new.

He sat beside her on the bed, watching, waiting, attuned to her unspoken needs. Paola hadn't planned to speak, but her defenses crumbled. She spoke of her mother, of a childhood taught to serve, to smile, to shrink. Love, she'd learned, meant adapting, dimming, enduring. She confessed to men who made her feel seen, only to vanish, leaving her hating herself for giving too much, hoping they'd reach her soul.

Alessio listened, his gaze holding her as if she were whole—not broken, not shameful. When he touched her, it wasn't sexual but reverent, his hands tracing her head and shoulders like a musician coaxing notes from a violin. Tears came unbidden, raw, born from someone touching the core of her loneliness.

"You're not broken," he whispered.

"You're carrying what isn't yours."

They didn't make love, though she'd expected it. He held her, kissed her forehead, and listened to her breath. That undid her more than passion could. At dawn, she left without goodbye, driving away, feeling hollow yet full, as if her pieces had been rearranged—not fixed, but transformed. She wasn't proud or ashamed. She'd entered a place where women paid for intimacy, not to find a man, but to meet herself. For the first time, she didn't flee what she found. She made a choice.

Chapter 25:

Luca's Ritual of Cleansing

Luca didn't know what he sought, only that he needed cleansing. At dawn, he stepped into the cold sea, its bite a confession, each wave carrying his guilt. He didn't swim but let the water hold him, washing away regret and the fragments of himself he'd lost. "I'm sorry," he whispered to the wind and waves. "To every woman who gave more than I deserved, every soul I touched without seeing."

He wept—not just for them, but for the boy he'd been, the man he'd become, for mistaking desire for worth, intimacy for performance. For Benedetta. For Paola. For the unintended marks he'd left. The sea embraced him, offering a flicker of forgiveness—for himself, for his blind path. A fragile hope stirred, whispering he could change.

Back in the city, he didn't call Paola. Instead, he wrote, words raw and trembling: Paola, I don't deserve a reply, but I must write. You were right—I wasn't honest with you or myself. I thought control was love, sex was power, and performance was closeness. Now I see something quiet, sacred, true. I offer my truth, without agenda or manipulation. I'm a man who loves you, not healed but healing, not clean but cleansing. I don't ask forgiveness, only a chance to speak in person. If not, know this: my imperfect love has changed me. I hope you're safe, whole, and well. With love, Luca.

He didn't expect a reply. For the first time, he was free of needing approval. He wanted her but released expectation, trusting fate. First, he had to face his pain, his shadows, to heal what was broken. Seeking guidance, he ordered a self-development book—a deliberate step toward the man he hoped to become. In that quiet act, the old Luca—burdened, defensive, lost—began to fade. A new Luca, aware, wounded, alive, emerged, ready to embrace truth. For the first time, he felt free, not because the past had changed, but because he had. Beyond the silence, he hoped Paola was safe, whole, well, believing change was possible—not for her, but for himself..

Chapter 26:

Smoke and Salt

Luca didn't know what drew him to the book. When the Body Shuts Down, the Soul Speaks promised insights into sacred sexuality, its cover like incense smoke trapped in glass. He hadn't read a book in years—only contracts, emails, and finance articles. But this title stopped him. From the first page, it spoke of Eastern philosophy: energy, when transformed, is never wasted. Soul, body, and mind are one—deny one, and the others suffer. Restrain not from fear but from wisdom, and life's energy gathers, reshaping the inner world.

The book told of a man in his fifties, chasing relationships, seeking validation, only to feel empty. Exhausted, he chose abstinence—no dates, no intimacy, no searching. At first, the silence was unbearable, like music silenced in a room where he'd danced blindly for decades. But within it, he heard himself—his breath, his truth. He rediscovered strength, boundaries, clarity. "Now I can love from fullness, not hunger," he realized.

Abstinence became a reset, a conscious choice. Without the pursuit of validation, his energy gathered—awareness sharpened, perception deepened. Sex transformed into an exchange, every touch leaving traces. Without stillness, he couldn't know his desires; without clarity, relationships mirrored confusion. Discipline and presence let his soul speak through breath, intuition, and feeling. Sensitivity became intelligence, not weakness.

Luca closed the book, silence settling around him—not empty, but alive. The words reshaped him, no longer a man driven by impulse but one gathering strength, focus, and clarity. His life had been automatic: desire, action, fleeting pleasure, repeat. Now, he felt choice—true choice—to act from wisdom, not hunger. Every touch had left traces, and he'd left pieces of himself, unaware. Awareness brought weight but also power to reclaim himself.

That night, he filled the bathtub with hot water, sea salt, Epsom salt, and a candle flickering nearby. He undressed, sank in, and whispered names into the steam: Tanya, Elisa, Caterina, the married one, the American actress, those whose names he'd never asked. And Paola. Not to release her, but to feel her absence's ache. Hands on the water, he spoke: "I release you. I return what is yours. I take back what is mine."

For thirty days, he contacted no one—no sex, no flirting, no calls to women who always answered. He silenced the chaos, rising at dawn to breathe. His body ached, not from abstinence but from the withdrawal of control, performance, and rush. Beneath it lay raw sadness—for years of taking without feeling. Yoga, meditation, and silence softened him. His hands no longer reached for his phone; his eyes no longer sought escape. One evening, in a café, an older woman caught his gaze—silver hair, laughter in her eyes, fully herself. He didn't speak, only watched, and something shifted. "This is it," he thought. "To see without taking." At home, he wept—not for loss, but for recognition. He wanted to apologize to Tanya, to confess his interest had veiled his emptiness. He didn't know if Paola would forgive him, but he no longer sought change to win her. He sought to become a man worthy of her—a man free of patterns that devalued women, that kept love conditional.

He envisioned a true partnership, built on trust, respect, and understanding. It couldn't come from fear, only faith. He vowed to listen, especially when it was hard. He began crafting a new life, not just a company, but a path aligned with his truth. A connection with Paola, rooted in respect, two souls meeting as equals. For the first time, he felt a sacred, unshakable power—not through control, but through integrity, love that simply was.

Patrizia realized his change but couldn't love him anymore. Too much pain lingered, dignity broken.

"You trust yourself now," she said.

"You don't need me anymore. Be here for our child."

With a check, she offered a fresh start—so their child could know a father to be proud of. This was no ending, but a beginning—a life reborn through clarity, courage, and truth. Luca understood that from this moment on, it was no longer about him. It was now company for Paola and his daughter—and for those who needed a chance: the inexperienced students, the older ones left behind, still searching for work. He wanted to become the kind of man whose presence carried quiet strength, whose silence could calm a storm, and whose kindness could alter the course of another's day. In that moment, something within him shifted—not suddenly, but like dawn breaking through the mist. Luca understood at last that meaning didn't come from pursuing his own happiness, but from being the reason someone else could hope again. With that realization, he felt truly alive—emotionally mature and ready to build a new company.

Lux Lucens
In Bed With Luca
Prime Enterprises Media 2025

For permission requests, please contact: info@primedia.cz
Prime Enterprises Media publishes this book on 24 July 2025 via Amazon Kindle Direct Publishing and other independent platforms.

www.primedia.cz[1]

---

1. https://www.primedia.cz/

www.ingramcontent.com/pod-product-compliance
Lightning Source LLC
Chambersburg PA
CBHW071127250626

47159CB00006B/2154